The Ultimate Betrayal

Danielle Walker

YJLM Publishing House
www.yjlm13productions.com

Printed in the United States of America

ISBN

ACKNOWLEDGMENTS

I would first like to thank my lord and savior Jesus Christ, for giving me this talent and love for writing. If it wasn't for him, none of this would be possible. I would like to thank my mom Carmela Walker, for always being there for me and listening to my craziness. When all I needed was for someone to listen. I would like to thank my brother Adrian Greene. For always being the backbone of our family and keeping me and my mom stable when we needed you. You really inspire me, more than you would ever know. I would like to send a special thanks to my grandmother Susan Walker(nana)(deceased) and my aunt Carlene McClendon. For always instilling 'books before boys, because boys bring babies', in me and my cousin Maleah Walker. Because without their influence, we wouldn't have made it as far as we have today.

I would like to send a HUGE shout out to my cousin Brittany Wright. This young lady has played a major part in my life, and I hers. Even though, I have sisters. She was raised with me as if she were mine. I would like to thank my dad Alvin Walker. For always keeping a positive attitude and boosting me up even when he didn't know it. Without his constant motivation, I would've never finished. I would like to send a special thanks to my best friend Tonika Ballard, for always being there no matter what. I could write a whole book on what this woman has done, still doing, and what she means to me. Because, through it all. Ups and downs. Without her, I know I wouldn't be where I am now. I love you Niqua! And a special thanks to everyone that wished me well throughout this entire experience.

I would like to take this moment and thank a few of my friends. All my ride or die divas, that have backed me and still are supporting me constantly. Jennifer Height, I could be with you anywhere. And we would turn a boring five minutes into the funniest experience a stranger or friend could have in a lifetime. Shannette Black, I could always count on you in those ISMG days to listen to my stories and make the time fly by. Jalisa Carter-Crawford, no matter what. No matter when. No matter where. No matter the time. No matter the crazy. She is always there for me. I can really say if I ever needed someone to ride with me. You were always the one to call. I love you Lisa. Reyellea Milton, not only are you a blessing from God. I thank God my dad married your mom, so we could be sisters. This has truly been the best twenty years of my life. Ever since we've met, we've been joint by the hip and it's always an adventure whenever we get together. Angel Walker, I thank you for my nephew. That's the best gift you could've ever given me. Every time I see him, my heart smiles. Keshawn Jones, I've known you since 6th grade and I could always come around your house and talk about anything and you the same. I'm still till this day mad Mrs. Judy married my man. But, that's Ok. They were a better match anyway.

I would like to thank my grandma Altha Dean Holloman, for helping me learn to be independent. By not always giving us everything we asked for. Even though, we pulled one over on you. By always sending Brittany in to ask you for the stuff we wanted (our secret weapon). It was fun aggravating you when you were left alone with us and when you were on the phone. Remember that time you were talking to Slappy and we were hiding outside your door, squirting you with the water gun and you thought it was a leak in the house (laughs). Good times, good times.

I would like to thank my great grandmother Lorene Williams(mother), for always being excited. No matter what it was I decided to do and I changed my mind frequently. You always were excited to hear the plan and never told me I was doing too much. You would just say 'ok'. And I really, really appreciate that. It was the belief you had in me that makes me thank God to have you.

I would like to send the biggest thanks to James Rainey(deceased). Over everyone I've mentioned in these acknowledgements. This man was a huge part of the woman I am today. Every time he came over to play cards with my grandma, work on the lawn, pick up my brother or uncle for work. Pick up my grandma, or just come over because he was bored. He always came to 'preach' (what Brittany called it) to us. He would constantly preach to us about school, grades, jobs, and debate with us kids. He would ask us a question and no matter how we'd answer. He would challenge it. We were never right. For some reason he was harder on me then he was on my brother and cousin. And when I finally turned twenty-one, he told me why. He stated, I was the laziest out of the three. But, he saw the most potential in me. He would nag me about my grades, because he knew I was just doing enough to get by and could do better if I applied myself. He was right. I never liked school. Whenever we'd bring home an 'A', he would give us money. So of course Brittany racked up. I could have, but I was always scheming on how I could get more then what he was offering. So I didn't waste my time. I gave him honor roll my senior year. Just to give him one thing cause I said he nagged so much, why not. I really wish he was alive today to see all I've done. I can hear him now nagging at me for not finishing college. But, I will eventually. Just to say I did it. You are missed Mr. Rainey.

I would like to send another special thanks to Bishop Robert Johnson(deceased). You knew me before I knew myself and when you died. I had to find me. You were that father figure in my life when my father wasn't, when I needed him the most. I could always come talk to you or call and talk about anything that bothered me. And you would listen and talk me through. I could tell you something and you wouldn't tell a soul. The way you guided us in our upbringing, shows still till this day in my character. And I thank you for that and your wife Barbra Johnson.

I would like to send my last thanks to Denim, who works at ACS. There are no words that I can use that can express how grateful I am to have met you. They say save the best for last and I had to save it for you. I thank you because when I first started writing. You would come and ask me 'how's the book coming'. Even when I only had one page and couldn't think of what to write next, you would constantly ask 'how's the book coming'. I can't tell you how many times from that first day I've re-wrote this thing. And when I finally thought I was done and I was releasing it that summer. My lawyer came and told me it still needed work. Ohhh the anger , stress, and agony. I'm going to personally purchase this book out of my own money, sign, and deliver it to you hand in hand. Why? Because I owe you this. Thank you!

The Ultimate Betrayal

CONTENTS

The Ultimate Betrayal

IT IS WHAT IT IS

An unbreakable bond, that was created instantly between two friends,
Can it withstand the test of time, or will it crumble under pressure?
As Shelly attempts to make a name for herself in the fashion industry, will
Jasmine allow her underlying jealously interfere
Or will she support her lifelong friend?
When loyalty has no limits, can these two best friends keep their
Sisterhood intact, or will this create a
Lifelong enemy..........

OH NO SHE DIDN'T

Ring! Ring! Ring!..... Ring! Ring! Ring!......

"Hello."

"Hi, may I speak with Bernard?"

"He's not here. Would you like to leave a message?"

"Naw, I'll call back." The unknown caller said with an attitude.

"Is this Shelly?" She continued to pry.

"This is she." Caught off guard. Shelly proceeded to answer. "And may I ask with whom am I speaking with?" Curious of who could have known her identity since she'd just moved in. *I wonder who this could be and how they know my name? It can't be one of his family members because they wouldn't have call private. And, why she got an attitude? This bitch.* Entertaining her subconscious thoughts.

"If you're not clear on who I am. I'm Bernard's ex-girlfriend who you called maybe eight to seven months ago, accusing me of messing with him. Even though, I told you I wasn't." Ranting in the phone as she motioned her hand back and forth. Like she was in a confrontation. "Umm yeah, because of that little stunt you pulled. I noticed Bernard may have not forewarned you of who I am." Talking smack as if she was the baddest thing smoking.

I can care less about who this bitch think she is. Shelly thought to herself as she glanced at the phone with a smug look on her face, before she placed it back to her ear.

"Well…. Since that night, because you pissed me off. I started back hanging with him."

Pissed you off! Appalled by her verbiage. *I like her nerve ….* Still debating with her thoughts as the anonymous caller continues to annoy.

"And we've been sexing and hanging out ever since. Just to let you know." Laying the icing on the cake.

They've been what! Considering hanging up in this callers face.

"He actually got angry." Pausing as she laughed. "Because I didn't come over on his birthday." Still giggling in the background. "Oh… And I was with him Valentine's Day as well….." Feeling there wasn't any competition concerning Mr. Curry.

I wonder how he found time to squeeze that in, because he was with me both times as well.

"Umm… Let me see. I spend the night every Monday and Wednesday. Therefore, I know when you're calling the next following Tuesday or whenever he doesn't answer."

That son of a bitch. Shelly gasp for air.

"I'll take the blame." Trying to be modest. "That's because he's with me." Thinking of more beans to spill. "We went out last Saturday. If you don't believe me; you can view my mobile pictures and you'll see him having fun at Destiny Mill."

She still carrying on. Shelly thought as she grew tired of hearing this grand confession.

"I spent the night this past Tuesday. Naturally we fucked. And I'm supposed to spend the day with him tomorrow."

Groupie… Shaking her head in disbelief. Thinking on how pathetic this

2

girl really is.

"We supposed to be going to the laundry mat and later to the Comedy Club. But, being I'm getting bored. You can have your boyfriend back."

LET'S MINGLE

"Girl….. Pass me the eye liner." Shelly asked as she motioned for her friend to place the pencil in her hand.

"Which one?" Unsure of which to choose. "The black one or the brown one?" Waving both in her hands.

"Black! Duh…" *I swear I believe this girl is slow sometimes. Don't she see what I got on? Then again, her matching skills do be off occasionally.* She chuckled.

"Ooo…. Do you think Arnez is going to be in the 'Spot' tonight?" Jasmine asked as she stared at Shelly, trying to anticipate her response.

"Are you serious?" Rolling her eyes, because she felt it was stupid of Jasmine to ask her such a rhetorical question. "Why wouldn't the owner be present in his own establishment?" Tracing her right under eyelid with the liner. In hopes of adding more depth to her appearance.

"True… But, that doesn't necessarily mean he shows up every night." Shrugging her shoulders to brush off the possibility of being disappointed.

"Look, what I'm having a hard time understanding is." Getting closer to the mirror. "Why you keep beating around the bush with this grown ass man?" Continuing to trace her eye. "All you have to do is open your mouth and tell him how you feel and that you would like to hang out sometimes."

Placing the pencil on the counter. "If he's interested." Looking around for her lipstick. "Things could just start from there."

"No!" Jasmine blurted out abruptly. "If he wants to date me." Pointing to herself. "Then he has to approach me first." Crossing her arms to make her decision final. "That's the way I was raised to believe. Therefore, that's just the way it its."

What world is this girl living in, because she defiantly need a welcome mat that has '20th Century' written all over it. Psycho.

"Riddle me this." Smearing her lips together to even out her lip stain. "How is the man supposed to ask you out, when he doesn't have the slightest idea of your liking him?" *Idiot.* "Every time he comes around, you act as if you have a nasty attitude!" *I mean come on now lady.* Rolling her neck as she awaited Jasmine's response.

"It's called 'read in-between the lines'." Clearing her throat. *She can't be serious.* Shaking her head as she listened to the words coming out of Jasmine's mouth.

"What lines are you expecting him to read between when they all have exclamation marks at the end of them. But enough of this chitter chatter it is what it is. I'm ready now. Let's go." *If I had to stand there and listen to that nonsense any longer, I probably would've popped.*

"Alright let me get my keys."

Walking out of the bathroom. Jasmine went to search her bedroom for her car keys, while Shelly finished gathering her things. Ever since Shelly introduced Jasmine to Arnez, she has had a little high school crush on him. But, because of her fear of rejection. She has kept it a secret between her and her best friend. Whenever he would speak to her. Even if it's just a gesture to say 'hello'. Jasmine would jump off a cliff to the point of no return.

"This girl right here." Shelly mumbled under her breath. "I tell you the truth." She continued.

"Damn!" Throwing the pillow down on the bed. "Where the heck did I put those keys?" Glancing around the room indecisively. "I can't find my keys Shell!" Yelling down the hall as she continued to fumble through the covers.

Dag'. Shelly thought. Trying to prevent herself from losing her balance after stomping her foot in the floor. 'Got to be more careful'. *I swear if this child wasn't my best friend, I would've been dropped her simple butt.*

"We'll take my truck then!" She yelled. Leaning on the door as she rubbed her left foot.

"Okay!" *At least, I get to save my gas for the week.*

Turning out the bedroom light. Jasmine grabbed her purse from the night stand and closed the door. Shelly overheard her coming down the hall. Therefore, she swiftly gathered her things and limped towards the door. Searching threw her purse for her keys. She finally found them at the bottom and proceeded to lock up. As Shelly unlocked the truck with the key pad, Jasmine slung her body in the passenger seat and buckled herself in. Throwing her purse in the back. She then glanced at Jasmine and turned the radio on as she shook her head in embarrassment.

"Oooh! That's my song!" Jasmine blurts out uncontrollably as she throws her hands in the air and grinds her body in her seat. "I don't want no bomb. A lame is a guy that can't get no love from me. Hanging on the passenger side of his best friends ride. Trying to get at me!" She sung while reaching to turn the radio up. Lost for words. Shelly ignored her friends enthusiastic behavior.

"Just make sure you're wearing your scrub shades when we pull up. Cause I'm defiantly not trying to spend my night ducking and dodging leaches." *I ain't got time for the broke-ness tonight.*

"Is Candice and Nichole hanging with us as well?" Jasmine asked. Calming down off her natural fumes.

"Yeah. They both text me earlier and said they're going to meet us in our usual booth."

"Cool." Making herself more comfortable as she relaxed in her seat. "I hope they got there early enough, so nobody got a chance to take our seats." *I better not catch nobody in my seat, or this will be a night to remember.*

"I'm pretty sure they're here already."

As Shelly pulled her SUV into the parking lot. She could sense this was going to be a wild night. The parking lot was jammed packed and it appeared to only have a couple vacant spaces over in the valet area. One thing's for sure, she wasn't parking in another lot down the block. And on top of that, she wasn't paying valet an arm and a leg to get a space either.

"Aye Jasmine."

"Yeah." Startled by the way Shelly called her name. She turned to see what she wanted with a confused look on her face, missing all of the eye candy passing by.

"Do you see any spaces on your side?"

"Yeah, I saw one. But it's over by the fire hydrant." Pointing out the window to direct Shelley's view. *She did all that. Just to ask me about a freaking parking spot.* Jasmine complained in her thoughts. Distracted by the all-white Royce that pulled in the lot. "I wonder who that is." Trying to see how many heads she can spot through the tent.

"Thirsty much?"

"Never that." Jasmine chuckled.

Searching for the vacant space Jasmine pointed out for her. Shelly saw a group of women crossing in front of her truck tip-toeing to the club. As a method of trying not to fall in their six inch heels. *Now they know. If you can't walk. Then, there's no need of playing yourself. But, I can't knock them for trying.*

"I saw that one when I turned in. But, if I park over there. We won't be able to get the doors open." *I ain't trying to scratch these doors. That may can fly with her vehicle, but not in mine.*

"We could climb out the back." Jasmine suggested as the truck became silent.

"Girl! Hell naw!" *She out her rabbit ass mind!* "I ain't climbing out this truck!" Frowning as though this was the most disrespectful suggestion she'd ever heard in her entire life. "What's wrong with you?" Questioning Jasmine as she gave her the evil eye. "We too old for all that! We ain't teenagers no more! This grown booty not teenage booty that will be in the air. If I climb over that seat, I'm liable to not be able to finish the roll!" *Crazy.*

"You stiff like that now?" She taunts jokingly.

"Who turn is it to pay for valet?" Ignoring Jasmine's attempts to make light of the situation. *I can't believe this helpha talking about climbing over some gosh durn seats. We ain't climbing over this leather. I don't care what the situation maybe. Not today.*

"I don't know why you're being so durn cheap. You know Toni will park that ass for free, if you let him ride that thang." She continues to joke. Laughing so hard snot slid out her nose.

"He ain't riding jack over here!" Shelly responded urgently as they laughed in unison.

"Do you have some tissue in here?"

"I think I have some napkins in the glove compartment." Still circling the lot. "That's what you get."

After finally finding a decent parking space. The girls made there entrance into the club. The place was packed and the dance floor was over crowed.

9

Before they had a chance to look around to see if they saw anyone they recognized "hey girls"! Someone shouted from across the room.

"Look there's Nichole." Elbowing Shelly and pointing in Nikos direction. From the look of things. They could tell she offed a few drinks already, because she appeared to be unstable as she stood by the booth.

"Hey boo. Is Candy here with you?" Shelly asked.

"Yea, she's somewhere around here talking to Rock." *There her hot tail go again.*

"You know they've been talking nonstop since that night he took her home." Stating in a gossiping way.

"I know. Mama said she keeps that line tied up so much, they had to make her get off several times last week." *Let that had been me. Daddy would've snatched my cord out the wall and dared me to buy another one.*

"Dag, I wonder what they be talking about." Jasmine butts in curiously.

"Whatever it is, she's sprung off of it." Shelly replied as everyone started laughing. "I know he took her to the park the other day."

"The park!"

"Stop hating Jazz dag!" (Teeth smacking in the background.)

"Yeah, the park."

"Ain't nobody hating!"

"I wonder what made him do that." *I wish somebody did that for me.* Shelly thought. "You know Candice always been on that sweet romantic type stuff. I'm just surprised she talked him into doing so."

"I know right." Nichole agreed.

There was no need for any of them to purchase any drinks, because they've been coming to 'The Spot' for several months now. And since Arnez and Shelly are good friends, everything was free. The food was right and the numbers were high on capacity. This was defiantly the place to be on a Friday night. The music was popping and everyone was having a good time. When all of a sudden, two 6'4 brown skinned fellas started making their way to the ladies table. None of which saw them as they were approaching. Everybody was having such a good time laughing at Niko's singing, that neither of them ever turned around to even notice.

"Good evening ladies." One of the gentlemen greeted.

"Where he come from?" Nichole leaned over, whispering to Shelly. Trying to be as discrete as possible.

"My name is Bernard Curry and this is my friend Michael Anderson." He introduced. Pointing to himself and then at Michael.

"Hi, I'm Jasmine. And these are my friends Shelly and Nichole." Smiling as she greeted him back. "What can we do for you fellas?" Tilting her head flirtatiously.

"Well, I saw your lovely friend here." Directing his attention to one of the other girls he was inquiring about.

"Thank you, I think your lovely to!" A drunken Nichole jumps up and interrupts. *Look at her drunk behind.* Shelly joked to herself.

"From the view of my V.I.P, and I had to come and ask if she would like to join me for a few drinks." Hoping to get a yes.

"Of course I would love to come join you and your………." Pausing as she taps her head as if something was going to pop out. "What he say your name was again?" She asked Michael as she waved her cup in a circular motion with bedroom eyes.

"And I was kind of hoping we could exchange numbers as well."

Little did the girls know, this was 'The Bernard Curry and Michael Anderson' which played for the 'SBA'. Both these gentleman were well paid. Not only were they paid. But, to top it off. They both were light on the eyes as well.

"Which friend were you referring to?" Jasmine asked with a bit of jealousy. Because she wanted someone to come over and inquire about her.

"If I'm not mistaken. You introduced her to me as Shelly." Contemplating, if he remembered her name correctly.

"That's that bullshit!" Nichole shouted. Swirling her cup in the air and flopping back down in her chair. "He know he wanted all this." Using her hands to outline her frame. "How could he not?" Talking to herself as she took a hard sip of her tonic. "DAMN!" Getting angrier by the second. "I done wasted some of my drank fooling with y'all helphas." She complained as she brushed the juices from her chest.

As the 'Y' in her name rolled off his tongue. Shelly's heart dropped to the pit of the empty stomach she was sitting on. Apparently, the DJ had to hear him speak her name as well. Because in her mind, the music stopped as soon as he did. She couldn't believe this tall, brown skinned, sexy caramel brother was here asking for her. Even though, Shelly is aware of her beauty. She still can be a little modest about it.

"Soooo, is it okay if I could call you sometimes?" Crossing his fingers behind his back. Hoping she don't embarrass him with the 'shut down' in front of everyone. Feeling a bit of hesitation, she agrees and gives him her number.

"Well ladies, it has been a pleasure meeting all of you. And I hope to be seeing you again real soon."

All eyes were glued to the fellas as they walked away from the table. No one saw them come. But, everyone watched them go. The girls were left speechless. Clueless to the thought of what just took place and stunned by the attractiveness of both gentlemen.

"Ohh, girl! He was fine!" Nichole shouted. Over emphasizing fine. *You can say that again.* "And his friend! Oh, girl! That friend!" She continued to lay it on thick as she caressed her knees. Like she was massaging a pain that couldn't be rubbed out.

"I know right." Shelly agreed.

"The way you were acting." Jasmine mocked. "I'd think you was in a desert or something because you shoal was thirsty!"

"I wonder what made him come over here and pick me." Doubting herself. "With all these other women in this club, including y'all. He chose me. Why?" Loss for words.

"Trick!" Shouting with the urge to haul off and slap the taste out of Shelly's mouth for saying something stupid like that. "If you don't stop that insecure junk and get with the freaking program!" She advised. "If you don't want him, I'd gladly step in and take him off your hands any day." *Oh no she didn't.* Shelly thought to herself as she watched her friend make a mockery of her distress.

"You always talking about you'd take somebody."

"Hell, because I will!" Niko admitted. "She actting like she don't want him." Pointing her unstable finger at Shelly. "All I'm suggesting is she move over for a real woman that will gladly step in and handle that business." Sipping on her margarita. Trying her hardest to preserve the last ounce. "Make it last forever..." She sung as she peered into her glass.

"Go get your own man!" Jasmine attacked.

"It's getting late girls and I'm all partied out." *Plus, you helphas done showed out for one night. I can't take no more of this petty drama.*

"But we just got here!" Pleading like a nine year old begging their mother to let them stay up an extra hour before bed.

"I know. But, I've gotten sleepy and I really need some rest. Business been a little hectic lately with all these late nights and early mornings. The stress has finally started taking a toll on a sister."

Yeah right. Nichole thought.

"Is it okay if Jazz catches a ride with you Candy?"

"Yeah, I guess so. Since she ain't got no other options and all." Full of sarcasm. "But, you know you wrong for ditching us."

"But you love me though." She teased. Laughing at her friends expense.

"Girl bye!"

"I'll call y'all later." Making promises while leaving the table.

'Okay'. They all sang harmoniously.

'Tonight was a nice girls night out'. Smiling as she walked towards her vehicle. Suddenly, Shelly felt her purse vibrate. She knew instantly it was her cellular phone, but the sensation caught her off guard. Fishing for it at the bottom, she was distracted by a sudden embrace from behind.

"Aye, lil mama."

'*Omgeezy*', she thought. As a chill came over her and fear of what was about to happen next crept in mind.

"When you gon' let me treat you somewhere nice, sweet thang?"
Shaken up a bit, Shelly muscled up enough courage to turn and see who her admirer was.

"Boy!" She shouted. "If you don't get your scrawny hands off me, I'm going slap the taste out your stupid mouth!" Angry, but relieved it was a face she knew instead of a strangers.

"Dang, shorty!" Fixing his clothes from the impact of the push Shelly delivered. "Why you always gotta be so rude to your boy?" *He got some nerve.* "All I wanna do, is treat you somewhere you ain't never been before." *How he know where the hell I've been and ain't been.* "And show you a side these other lames ain't trying to show you." Wanting to make a good impression of himself to her.

'I ought to'... Restraining the urge to wop him with her purse.

"Toni, don't nobody want you!" Clutching her purse closer to her bosom. "Where's my keys!" She yells as she snatches them out of his hand.

"See you next week!" Smiling as he watched her walk away. "Um, um, um, um, ummm." He grunted.

"Fuck off!" Giving him the middle finger as she walked to her car.

"She wants me." He chuckled. As he walked towards the entrance of the club, continuing to give the customers their keys as they exit.

"I'm happy it was Toni and not somebody else. I almost pissed myself, fooling around with that boy. Don't he know he can't be walking up on people like that this time of the night. He don't know what I could've had in this purse. Hell, I don't know what he could've had on his mind. Let me hurry up and get my butt in this truck." Shelly spoke to herself aloud as she scurried to her vehicle.

After meeting Bernard at 'The Spot'. He and Shelly started dating within the next few weeks. Eventually he revealed to her the profession he works. And she later tells him she is a fashion designer and she has her own line out as well.

"I know it's only been seven months since we first started dating but I was wondering. If you wanted to of course." Feeling sure of himself. "Would you like to move in with me?" *Say what......* Never saying it, but her facial expression said it all. "I have more than enough room for the both of us, so it wouldn't be any complaints regarding space. It really would be nice to have you to come home to and not an empty space." *Awe, how sweet....* Feeling butterflies in her stomach. "Instead, of us always jumping house to house."

He does make a good point about that jumping around thing. And it would save on gas. But who's counting pennies. She joked. *Forty-five dollars every four days just to come back and forth for some dick. Not me...*

"What you think about that?" Feeling as if he's the star of a soap on daytime television.

"I know everything's been going well for us. And it's not that I don't want to live with you. Trust me I do. It's just, this my first house and I'm not ready to move out of it unless I'm married and my husband and I purchase one together." The shutdown. "I'm very flattered that you want to live with me. But, I'm going to have to refuse the offer right now bae." *Did she really just tell me no.... This woman been having me walking on egg shells since the first day we've met. Why she just won't act like regular chicks and say 'yes' to everything. It's always a mystery with her. But, what can I say. I think I love her.*

"I understand." Bernard says disappointed. But, in a way where she couldn't pick up on his disappointment. "Are we still on for dinner with the crew tonight?" Throwing the attention off his transparent emotional state. *Do she realize how many women would kill for their men to ask them to move in with them. Let alone, for me to ask them that... Who does she take me for?*

"Yeah, let me call Niko and make sure everybody's still on the same page time wise." She replied as she arose from the sofa.

"Okay, well I'd see you later then." Stretching as he stood. "I have a few things I need to go and take care of before we head out." Leaning in to kiss her on the cheek before he heads for the door.

"And bab." He turns around grabbing the door handle.

"Yeah." Giving off a nonchalant vibe.

"I love you."

"Awww, I love you to pooda."

Finally alone, Shelly walked through the bedroom to start her search for an outfit for that evening. She thought to call Jasmine and Nichole to make sure their plans hadn't changed for the night. But, she couldn't decide who to call first.

'I wonder if these helphas still going', walking around the bed to retrieve her phone from the night stand. 'Let me call Jazz real quick.'

"Hello."

"Hold that thought, let me click Niko in."

"Hello."

"What's up? Are we still on for 'BIC'S' tonight?"

"Yeah, I'm still coming. And, I'm bringing a surprise guest." Jasmine replies. Prolonging her response to savor the fact that she had a date.

"Oh really." Stunned by the sudden news update. "And why are we just now hearing about this surprise?" Shelly asked.

"Because I asked him to keep our relationship under wraps. At least, until I felt I was ready to tell everyone."

"Say what!" Nichole blurts out in disbelief. "A relationship! He must be ugly or something and you're to embarrass to bring him around us?" She joked. "Cause ain't no way you're in a relationship and we ain't heard nothing about it."

'See this why she probably ain't told us nothing'. Shelly mumbled under her breath.

"No. I just didn't want you nosey helfas all in my business. Asking me all these questions like you doing now, yet." *Who she calling nosey...* "Defiantly, if I wasn't sure myself what would become of this thing we call ourselves starting." Jumping in a defensive mode.

"Well the least you could do is tell us when and where y'all met."

This trick ain't giving up none of the juice. If it was one of us, she would be all over our crotches trying to sniff out every single detail she could get.

"In due time, all will be revealed." Jasmine says as she hangs up her end of the line. *Who she thinks she is, Mufasa or somebody?*

17

Still in shock, Shelly couldn't believe her best-friend had been keeping this secret from her. When in the past, she has always kept it one hundred with her at all times.

"I can't believe she's been dating somebody and have kept it secret this long." Shaking her head in disbelief.

"I know."

"That just makes me more anxious to meet up." Bouncing up and down like a crack feign, itching for another hit.

"Me too." Still giving short answers as if she didn't really care. Growing restless with Niko, for not responding with the feedback she was looking for. Shelly went ahead and rushed her off the phone.

"I'd see you in a few." Rolling her eyes.

"Alright then Shell, see you in a bit."

Curious of who the mystery guest could be. Shelly picked up the pace. 'Finally', she assured herself. As she pulled out a nude colored dress and laid it across the bed. She started smiling at the thought of Nard asking her to move in with him. 'He loves me'. Chuckling as she continued to powder her face. 'I think I'll wear the royal blue pumps with this. It speaks more to me then the red ones'. She knew her colors. Therefore, she knew this was defiantly an eye catcher. 'Black is not an option tonight'.

Since Shelly and Bernard agreed to take separate cars. He was already there awaiting her arrival when she pulled up.

"Good evening Mr. Curry. Majority of your guest have already arrived and have been seated in there designated seating areas sir." A flamboyant man greeted them as they entered. "If you would just follow me. I can show you to your party and get you seated as quickly as possible." As he led them around the other customers that were standing in line waiting to be seated.

Shelly couldn't believe what she saw. He was wearing a loud green bow tie, with black polka dots. Greeting everyone as they came in. As Shelly approached the table, she noticed Arnez sitting next to Jasmine. Before she could greet anyone. Michael blurts out 'dang B, you didn't tell me Jazz and Arnez hooked up'.

"This is as much of a surprise to me as it is for you brah." Shrugging his shoulders as if to say 'I didn't know'.

"Ha, ha, haaaa." He laughed.

"What's so funny?" Nichole asked. Interrupting as she makes her way around the table, hugging everyone in her path.

"Oh nothing honey. We're just making fun of Jazz and Arnez." Shelly gladly filled her in.

"Okay, so this the mystery guest." Trying to hold her own chuckles in. "How did this come about?" Getting more interested in the potential gossip she could make of this.

"Don't worry about all of that. Just know it happened and we're together." Flaunting as she leans over and start kissing her new boo.

"Well excuse me ma'am."

"You're excused." Giving her confirmation to butt out her personal.

"Has anybody ordered yet?" Skimming over the menu, trying to decipher what's good and what sounds like it may taste like crap.

"Yea, we all decided to go with the house special." Shelly helped. "Since they have such a huge selection to choose from, we all agreed on trying that."

"Why do these particular restaurants always got to have a house special?" She stated flipping through the menu. "I mean what's up with that? Can a sister get a variety?" Getting more dissatisfied with the chicken specials they had listed. "I guess since everybody eating it...... I'll eat it to." Sighing in disappointment. "At least I know if it's nasty. I won't be the only one in a fast food drive-thru once we leave." Laughing as she passed the waiter her menu.

In the mist of eating and discussing the game Nard and Mike played the night before. Bernard phone starts to vibrate. As he looked to see who was calling. He then excused himself from the table.

"Well, since everyone is here. I guess I can give you guys the big news." Receiving empty stares from around the table. 'I know she is not about to say she's pregnant'. Shelly thought as she braced herself for this bomb dropping.

"I GOT MY PROMOTION BITCHES!" Jasmine screams. Loud enough that every guest in 'BIC'S' attention was now directed towards her. 'Whew'. A sigh of relief came from the other side of the table.

"Call me G.M now!" She yells.

"Congratulations." Niko congratulated as she motioned for her drink. "It's about time they promoted yo ass." *There's always a hater in the bunch.* "You've been there for a year and a half now. They should've been gave you a promotion." She continues to taunt as she lifts her fork to stuff her face. "Hell, a raise to!"

"Damn Niko! Why you always hating on somebody? You ain't never got nothing good to say."

"Yeah, why so sour?" Shelly chimed in as well.

"Ain't nobody hating!" Taking offense to the accusations directed her way. "I'm just stating facts. It's about time." Bluntly stating as she tossed her fork down on her plate.

Twenty minutes had flown by and Bernard finally makes his way back to the table. Noticing the time difference, Shelly became curious of who the caller could have been.

"Baby."

"Yeah."

"Who was that on the phone?" She asked innocently. Trying not to alarm him of her insecurities.

"Just a little business I had to handle nothing major." Fanning her off as he attempted to steal a kiss to distract her from the obvious.

"Business had you gone for twenty minutes?" Irritated with him always referring to things as 'business' lately.

"You know how these things can get baby. Business is business. Just chill out." He assured her, picking over the cold food on his plate.

"Well, dinner was great." Speaking for the first time this evening. "I really enjoyed coming out with you guys tonight." Arnez said as he arose from the chair he had been occupying. "I should consider doing this more often."

"Yeah, it was."

"Yeah….. Well, I guess if I don't see any of you anytime this week. I know I will defiantly catch you all at the club for sure."

"Good night everyone." Giving her farewells as she stuffed a piece of chicken in her purse.

"Good night." The entire group sang.

"Make sure you call me Jasmine!" Shelly announced as she watched the chicken disappear.

"I will." Looking to see what else she could grab.
While walking to his car. Bernard motioned for Mike and pulled him to the side so no one could hear what he had to say.

"Man, I need to tell you something. But, I'm going to wait till practice tomorrow." With a 'I got something huge to tell you bro' look on his face.

"What's it got to do with?" Growing curious. But, not so much because you never know with Bernard.

"I can't go into details here, but we can discuss it when the setting is a

21

bit more private." Looking around to make sure no one was close enough to hear what he said.

"Alright then, I'll see you tomorrow." *With his paranoid ass.*

"Bet."

Since Shelly made the decision not to move in with Bernard. They drove their own cars to the restaurant. Shelly wasn't quit ready to part ways so soon, being she had a long week. She wanted a little more time with her boo.

"Bay, are you coming over tonight?" Hoping to take full advantage of the buzz she got from her drinks.

"Not tonight Shell."

Say what…... She thought. Unbelieving of the words she was hearing.

"I have to rest up for practice in the a.m., but I'll call you later on tomorrow okay."

I just know he didn't throw that practice line on me. I know he ain't sleepy. So what's really going on.

"Ok, well give me a hug and I'll talk to you later." She said disappointedly. *I'll let him slide this time. But, if he don't call me tomorrow. The cat will be out the hat on that ass.*

Checking her watch, Shelly noticed it was still kind of early. Therefore, she decided she would go visit her mom. 'I wonder what mama and the girls are up to'. She said as she started her ignition. 'I'll do a quick drive by'. Driving over to her mothers. The lights from the cars coming in the opposite direction made her feel like her life was flashing before her eyes. Reason being, with every new light. She had a flashback of random scenarios when Bernard mentioned 'it was business' to her. Walking in the house she saw her mother sitting on the couch watching television. The door was unlocked, so there was no need of knocking. Which was a bad habit the family had.

"Hey, ma." She greeted.

"Hey Shell." Surprised to see her walk through the door. "What brings you this way, at this time of the hour?" Glancing at the clock posted above the entertainment center.

"Oh, nothing." Swinging her purse on her left shoulder. "I was in the area and wasn't ready to go home yet. So I swung on by." *She know it ain't that late.* "Where're the girls?" Anxious because she hadn't seen them in a week.

"Well, Antoinette is over one of her girlfriend's house. You know this their spring break and Candice is in the room on that durn telephone again."

I could've figured that. She mumbled under her breath.

"Lord knows that child eat and sleep on that thang." Picking up the remote. "She needs to pay the bill, since she keeps it tied up so much." She continued to ramble as she tuned back into her show.

"Oh, okay. I'll go harass her for a bit." Making her way down the hall since her mother wasn't paying her any attention any longer.

Bursting in the room, Shelly saw Candice rolling around on the bed smiling like the cat off that wonder something movie. She couldn't resist the urge to mess with her. Yeah, she was happy for her sister. But the kid in her was ready to attack.

"Who you talking to?" She questioned using the best male interpretation she could muscle up.

"Rock!" She snapped.

"Oh, so you cheating on me now?" Trying to keep her voice from cracking. Shelly had to cover her mouth a few times, so she wouldn't blow her cover. Because it was too funny.

23

"Girl stop it I say. What you want?" 'This chick is out her marbles' whispering in the receiver.

"GIRL! Who you calling GIRL?" Snickering but still maintaining a perfect performance.

"Baby, that ain't nobody but Shelly!" Pleading with Rock.

"BABY! Who you calling BABY?" Taunting her sister the more. (Click.)

"Why you playing?" A whiny Candy asked. Confused on why her sister was being so mischievous.

"Ain't nobody playing with you! Get off the phone damn it!"

"You play to durn much man! What you want?" Yelling out angrily when she realized her boo hung up on her.

"Nothing, just wanted to come up here and mess with you before I went home." Admitting innocently.

"Uggghhhh…" (Exhaling.) "Where you coming from?" Finally giving in to Shelly's tantrum for attention.

"All of us got together and went out for dinner tonight." Waving her hand in the air as to say 'oh it was nothing'.

"Who is all?" *I like they nerve. And I like hers to, for not bringing me something back to eat.*

"Just the usual group. Nard, Mike, Cole, Jazz, Arnez, and I." She sighs.

"Arnez, what he doing there? And where did ya'll go?" Leaning over on the bed as she propped her head in her hands. Awaiting her sister to spill the beans.

"Gurl….." Sucking her teeth and snapping her fingers. "We went to 'BIC'S'. Apparently, he and Jazz supposed to have done hooked up." Giving neck action as she gave her the juice.

"Say whaaatttt!" Mouth open, eyes wide, and hands flat on the bed.

"Yeah girl. That's what I said when I found out." With both hands placed on her hips agreeing with Candice's reaction.

"And, why wasn't I invited?" Candice asked as she rolled off the bed to sit in an upright position.

"Cause you broke! That's why, duh!" Laughing at her sisters expense.

"Whatever…"

"What you got going for tomorrow?" Shelly asked.

"Nothing but class, why?" Trying to figure if she should've said she was busy.

"Let's go to the spa. I got you."

"Okay. Sounds like a plan to me." Getting excited from the thought of total relaxation for an hour at no cost to her.

"Well, I'm finna head on home. I'd see you in the morning. Love you."

"Love you to."

As Shelly hung her jacket in the closet. She noticed the red light blinking from her telephone. 'I wonder who this is' she thought. Pushing the 'check message button'. Her messages were played back instantly. "You have one unheard message." The answering machine recording announced as she closed the closet door. "Bitch, I hope you made it home safely." *Oh lord.* "You could've at least texted and let somebody know you made it." *Her loud ghetto ass.* "Bernard must be over there." *I knew she couldn't say one thing without being nosey.* "He probably is with all that liquor you threw back tonight. You lucky I'm in a good mood, or I would've come unglued on that ass for not letting somebody know you made it home." *She ain't finished yet… Geesh..* "Alright then girl, call me." *Ugghh……About dag blame time.* "Message received at 10:57 p.m. from 671) 873-2519." *That girl know she a mess and a half. I still can't believe her and Arnez hooked up. I wonder who made the first move. Oh, well. I know she'll spill the beans eventually. Ain't no need for me to even ask.*

JASMINE

The dew was settling in on the freshly cut lawn and you could hear the sound of the birds singing their morning hymns. The sun hadn't yet showed its face, but you could see the light breaking through the dark sky. Popping out of bed. Jasmine rushed through her morning rituals she would usually follow for getting dressed, because she was fifteen minutes behind schedule. Since this was her first official day of school. Being cute was extremely important. However, being on time out weighed appearance any day.

"I can't believe it's my first day already. It came so fast." Thinking out loud as she rushed through the parking lot. "I can't wait to meet some new people." She said to herself as she walked past the statues in the breeze way of her new campus. "Let me see what my first class is." Stopping to pull her backpack off.

Scrambling through her notebook. Jasmine pulled out a piece of paper that had 'schedule' written on top of it. Even though, this was indeed her first day. Her book bag was already a hot mess. "College Algebra with Dr. Greene at 8:30 a.m., cool." She said joyfully. *I wonder if it's a lady or a dude....* She thought. *I need to make a mental note to clean this dog gon' bag. Geesh...*

"It really don't matter. I just hope whoever it is, take it easy on us this semester." Thinking about how tough she'd heard some of the instructors to be. "Let me start searching for this classroom. I can't be marked late day one." Trying to discipline herself. "At least, if I'm on time this first week. That will give me a chance to be late next week." She joked. "Fake it till you make it."

After finding her class Jasmine looked around the room to see if she could spot any vacant seats. After a quick glance she noticed one on the back row next to a girl with long jet black hair. As she squeezed down the isle, giving her apologies for bumping individuals along the way. Jasmine scoped the rest of the attendees out as she passed. "This is going to be a tough group to connect with." She thought. One seat away, she contemplated if she should speak to her neighbor or wait until she spoke first.

"Hey, my name is Jasmine. What's yours?" She greeted. Sticking her hand out as she stared her neighbor in the face.

"What's up. My name is Shelly. Nice to meet you." Stretching her hand out to meet hers for a shake, hoping her palms weren't sweaty.

"Thanks, you to."

Taking a seat. Jasmine started unloading her books on the desk and pulled off her jacket. 'Could this class get any hotter'. She said to herself, struggling to get her right arm free of the sleeve. 'Finally', balling the jacket up and stuffing it in her bag.

"Is this your first day or are you a returning student?" She leaned over to ask Shelly.

"Na, this my first day." Barely looking up to acknowledge Jasmine. *Damn she nosey*. Shelly thought. Being she's not usually the friendly type. 'I hope this girl ain't trying to make new friends. Cause now ain't really the right time. I'm too sleepy for this ish right here'.

"How about yourself?" Asking because she didn't want to come off rude.

"This my first day as well. Hell, I was almost late." She joked. Fishing for her pencil.

"Me too." She chuckled.

"It's Shelly right?"

"Yeah."

"Do you have your textbook yet?" Anticipating her response.

"Yeah, I got it last week." Trying to avoid eye contact. *I knew that was coming. I hope she don't ask me what I think she's about to ask me.*

"Do you mind if I share with you today? I have to wait after class to get mine." Bating her eyes, trying to look as innocent as possible.

I knew this shit was about to happen. It never fails. Shelly thought. *Folks don't never come to school prepared.* Kicking the leg on the backside of the chair in front of her. *Soon, she gon' be asking to borrow a pen.* Grinding her teeth. *Then a scan-tron, then some paper, and then my cell phone.*

"Sure, I don't see why not. I don't mind." Forcing a smile on her face.

"Thanks."

"No biggie." *Uggghhh....*

As Jasmine continued to make herself comfortable. She looked up and saw the man she never thought existed. 'Damn' she mumbled.

"Damn, he fine!" Getting even more excited as she leaned over and elbowed Shelly to direct her attention towards the door.

"Girl, girl, girl, girl, girl." Rubbing her hands down her leg, so hard that if it was carpet. She'd have carpet burn. "I got to have him on my team!" She stated. Staring at her victim. Imagining him being a piece of bar-b-q chicken, she couldn't wait to lick the sauce off of. "Just wait. You're looking at my future right there." Boasting to Shelly, as she wiped the drool from her bottom lip. While looking around the room at her peers hoping no one saw her.

Lost in the sauce, Shelly shook her head and smiled. She had other pressing issues to focus on besides some guy. With a little investigation, Jasmine found out the fellows name was Mario Wright. And from that day forward she knew she would do whatever it took to make him hers. After class, Jasmine made it her business to go and introduce herself to the stud. Just so she could ask him for his telephone number.

"Hello, my name is Jasmine Rodriguez." Sticking her hand out to greet his. With a huge grin on her face. "And yours?" Flicking her eyes and twisting her right foot side to side to redirect her nervousness elsewhere.

"What's good ma." Sliding his tongue across his teeth. "I'm Mario, but my friends call me 'Man'." Rubbing his chin as he sized her up.

"Well 'Man'. I know this is our first day and all. But, I was kind of wondering if you were interested. Would you like to call me sometimes?"

"Yeah, I could do that." Reaching in his pocket for his cell. "What's the number?"

Jasmine's stomach was in knots, because she thought he was going to shut her down. She blurted her number out like the warden was doing roll call.

"It's 671) 873-2519." Not caring how anxious she appeared. Her main goal was to snag and bag him. And throwing bait was what she intended on doing.

"Alright, I'll hit you up a little later lil mama."

"That's what's up." Trying to sound cool and hip to the street slang. Knowing good and well, she was from the burbs.

As Jasmine continued to drool over her new catch as she watched him walk away. Shelly came out of the classroom and started interrogating her.

"Damn girl! You're moving a little fast ain't you?" Looking surprised because she didn't think Jasmine would move so quickly. "You ain't even been here two whole hours yet. Let alone, seen what the rest of your classes looking like and you already all over this man." *Fast ass*. Shelly thought. Making her judgment off first impressions.

"When you know, you just know girl." She advised.

From that moment on Jasmine and Shelly became inseparable. What better way to meet a friend, then off differences of opinions.

"I still think you tripped out for doing that."

"You'll live." Fanning her hand at a judgmental Shelly. As she stood completely still in the middle of the hall. "I'll see you Wednesday."

"Alright then."

Done for the day, Jasmine made her way to the bus stop. Along side a few other classmates, which were walking in the same direction. But, she didn't bother speaking to any of them. For she figured since she'd made a friend already, one was enough for that day. Focusing her attention on her footsteps, Jasmine was startled by a black Crown Vick that pulled alongside her.

'Ahhh, shit' she thought.

"Aye lil mama." The guy shouted from his passenger window. "You need a ride?"

Disturbed, Jasmine took her time turning around to tell the stranger 'no thanks'. Nervous, she muscled up enough courage to face her admire. When she got a full glimpse of the guy, she noticed it was Mario. Relieved to see a familiar face. Jasmine proceeded with the conversation gracefully.

"I should've known that was you." Trying to play coy. "With that accent and all." Blushing at him as she admired how nice of a vehicle he was driving. "I think I'd take you up on that offer."

"You can put your stuff in the back." He stated. While leaning over to open the door for her.

"Thank you."

"You're welcome ma." Propping back in the upright position as he reached over his shoulder to buckle himself in. "I got a few places I need to go, before I can drop you off at your destination." Advising her as he kept his eyes focused on the road; awaiting the stop light to change. "Is that alright with you?" Coincidently, staring her in the eyes.

Realizing she doesn't have a choice in the matter either way. Jasmine tried her hardest to say something, but she didn't want it to come off 'lame'. It was already out of her character to hop in the car with strangers. Because he was one of her classmates, she figured it would be okay to make this one time exception. Therefore, Jasmine dared to be adventurous for the first time in her life.

"Yeah, that's fine." Rubbing her palms together to smooth away the sweat. "As long as you're buying dinner." Making attempts to flirt. "Then, I think I can suffer through this country ride."

"I got you ma." Glancing out his rearview mirror, looking to see if anyone was following them. "That's not a problem." Cracking a smile. "I must admit. You caught me off guard this morning after class."

"How so?" Shifting her body towards him.

To him it would give the allusion she's giving him her undivided attention. But, in reality. It was her way of admiring how handsome he was without being creepy.

"I wasn't expecting you to come at me like that. I assumed you were about to ask for directions or something."

"Really…" Shying away from showing her excitement.

"Yeah." Still surprised. Almost choking on his own spit. "I have to say. That confidence thing you got going, is mad sexy yo. And I'm dig'n it hard ma."

Unsure of what choice of words to use next. Jasmine just blushed and glanced out the passenger window in complete silence. 'I can't believe he thinks I'm sexy'. She said to herself in her inner thoughts. 'Hold up. Did he really call me sexy or is he referring to my actions only? Hummm... I don't care. He still said it regardless'.

Feeling butterflies in her stomach. Jasmine tried to take her mind off them and relax. Cruising down Reeveland Avenue, she began to notice his stops weren't the regular 'hi' and 'byes'. She knew instantly. She was dealing with a drug dealer and he wasn't moving any light weights. Which was cool with her, because the only thing she could see were dollar signs. After had been driving around for several hours. Mario finally got hungry.

"What you got a taste for ma?" He asked as he closed his door.

"I'm not sure." She shrugged. "Whatever you choose is ok with me."

"You like wings?"

"Who doesn't?"

I see she got a smart mouth. Sucking his teeth. *That ain't gon' fly for too long.* He said under his breath. "Well, we can pick up some wings and head to my place for a bit. If that's alright with you, of course." Giving her an opportunity to say no. Even, if the option wasn't on the table for her to decide.

"That's fine." Replying hesitantly, being they'd just met a few hours ago. But, because she wanted to be adventurous. Jasmine had to go with the flow, regardless of her intuition warnings.

Stepping in the foyer, Jasmine was amazed by the view. His house was nothing compared to the way she envisioned it. The images she created were amateur to the actual layout. The kitchen was decked with marble counter tops. The living room was covered with plush white carpet. Every step she took, her feet would sink to the pit of the never ending depth of beauty. The walls were covered with fishes, because there were fish tanks built into both sides. Therefore, it gave the illusion of walking in an aquarium. The first thing Jasmine noticed when she came in the house. Was Mario's gigantic entertainment center that he had sitting in the middle of the living room floor. The surround sound was so lavish. He even had a projector hanging from the ceiling, so he could watch satellite television from it.

"Wow...... Is this all yours?" She asked. As she continued to admire the nick knacks he had plastered on the coffee table.

"Yeah, I cop'd this when I first settled in this city." Talking like it wasn't a big deal to him. He wasn't new to this lifestyle. He was true to this lifestyle. "I needed something real smooth." Kicking off his shoes, while he locked the door.

"This is nice...."

"I guess." He replied nonchalantly. "It's actually smaller then my other place I had back in Philly." He admitted. "Since this a buyer's market. I was like 'fuck it why not'."

"Did you have help choosing the location or did you do this on your on?" Getting straight to the answer she was looking for.

"Naa, shorty." He chuckled. "This all me."

"Okay, okay. I see ya." Shaking her head as she continued to focus her attention on the pictures he had hung on the wall. Basic art work for decoration purposes only. Once dinner was finished, they watched television awaiting their food to digest. After several hours had passed, Jasmine looked down at her watch and noticed time had flown by fairly quick.

"Whoa!" She said.

It was already 8:30p.m and Mario had been asleep for forty-five minutes now. Thinking he needs to wake up, she shrugs him.

34

"Mario."

"Humm." He grunted.

"It's late and I need to get home." Looking at him as he turned his back towards her.

"Umm hum."

"Get up." She continued to push on him. "I have an early class in the morning and I don't want to be late." She explained. "This will be my first day in that class. Get up!"

As Mario opened his eyes and yawned. He slowly started caressing her leg. Lusting in his mind the things he planned on doing to her. Gently easing his way up her thighs. He rolls over on her and leans in to plant his first kiss.

'I just know he didn't kiss me without asking'. Jasmine reflected to herself. 'And have the nerve to do it without brushing his teeth.' She thought. But, she never pushed him away. Deep down, Jasmine wanted to tell him no. But, the flutters in her stomach distracted her from doing so. Plus, her body was screaming for him to keep going.

Thrusting herself on top of his masculine body. She moaned with every encounter their lips had. Because he could smell the scent of her perfume, Mario's erection grew larger from just a whiff.

Removing her top, Mario continued to suck on her neck to make sure he didn't give her any chances to change her mind. Because he was so skilled in this profession and pleasing the body was one of his favorite expertise. He popped her bra strap with his left hand, while he caressed and sucked on her breast with his right.

Mario was extremely experienced and by the grip he had on her, Jasmine knew she wasn't dealing with no rookie. Not knowing what to expect from this encounter. One thing she could be certain of, this sex craved nympho was about to take her on a thrill of a lifetime.

Upon the first initial penetration. You could hear the sound of Jasmine gasping for air. She couldn't believe how big his nature was and became more excited with every deep stroke that followed.

"Damn, this pussy tight." He whispered to her as he took his time winding in her warm juice box. He knew it was going to be good, but he wasn't prepared for it to be this good.

In and out he stroked as she gripped his shoulders and drove her nails down his back. His mouth started to water as he slowly eased his man man back in to meet her peak.

"I can definitely fuck with this on a regular." He confirmed. Shifting his brain into focus mode, so he could control his substance.

Mario's mission was to take her down. Dividing and conquering her pussy was what he intended on doing. With that being his angle, there were no limits to the things he was prepared to do.

Faster and faster he stroked when the sounds of their bodies clapping together caught his attention. Pleased, he continued to jerk until he caught a Charlie Horse on his right side. But, regardless of the pain. He pulled through the fight. For he felt, he deserved this round of applause.

"Damn…. That ass phat." He said. Admiring her silhouette from behind. Tapping lightly with his hand. Causing her ass to jiggle like a bowl of jell-o.

The harder he jerked. The more excited he became. After witnessing the white juices engulf his penis. Mario creatively turned this into a game of 'peek-a-boo'. But, he called it. 'Hide that dick, make this bitch cum'. Sweat rolled down his back from the heat they created between them. Before either of them could inhale, Jasmine exhaled screaming out in pleasure.

To her it felt like his penis had a curve. So, whenever he penetrated her. It seemed to dig into the upper foundation of her vagina. Therefore, constantly creating a forceful friction in that area. Because it was a sensitive spot for her, Jasmine's body couldn't handle the sensation any longer. So much so, that it caused her back to arch uncontrollably and her walls to clamp down on Mario. She lost complete control of her breathing, to the point she couldn't think to inhale or exhale. The force of this reaction caused her toes to curl. Popping one by one as her hands gripped the sheets. She bit her lip and thrusted her body back into his pelvis like a mad woman.

Jasmine had never experienced a man hit every corner or even the peak of her Pandora box all in one stroke. She was thrilled and ready to take on more of whatever he had to give. As this session began to come to an end. Mario leans in and whispers in her ear.

"Jay baby."

"Ummm." She moaned. Licking her lips, eyes closed, mind clear, and focused on the thickness he continued to bless her with.

"Stay with daddy tonight and I promise I'd have you home and in class on time tomorrow." He asked.
The sound of his voice and the tone he used sent chills up her spine.

"Pull my hair and ask me again, daddy." She said. In the sexiest way any woman could ever say something to a man with his dick still sliding against her walls. Slow, but steady.

Aroused he placed his left hand on her stomach and twisted his right around her hair. Tilting her body towards him with her back arched just enough so she could hear what he had to say. Dominating her with every move to signify who's in charge, making sure their roles in this game was understood. Eliminating having to say who's duties were what. He gently yanked and stuffed. Pacing every breath as he focused on the sensation he felt from the penetration.

"Ahh." She moaned.

"Stay with me." He mumbled as he slowly packed every inch he had to stuff in her.

"Yes." She replied. Focusing on the friction between her legs as she flickered her clitoris with her right hand.

"I don't hear you." Pulling harder.

"Yes." Feeling a tickling sensation flow from where their bodies connected down her leg.

"I'm still unsure of what you said." He argued. "I heard a stutter." Getting aggressive because he enjoyed the squishy dialog his dick and her cat was having.

"Yes!" She screamed. As he stroked and pulled harder until they climaxed and stiffened. Tied to one another. 'Okay'.......

Rushing to find something to wear. Jasmine raided her bedroom to find a shirt to match her jeans. Because she was pressed for time, she only had time to take a wash up and gargle. It wasn't normal for her to skip brushing her teeth, but thank mankind for the creation of mouth wash. When she got back into the car, she noticed Mario had fallen asleep on the steering wheel. But, once she slammed the door. He woke right up.

"You ready?" He asked. Wiping the drool from his lip.

"Yeah."

Jasmine tried to get a little nap in before they arrived at the school. After the night they'd had and the long day she had on her agenda. Twenty minutes would be a reward for her. When he pulled in. Jasmine felt the impact from the ride over the speed bump as they entered.

"Damn it." She mumbled as she rubbed her head.

"What's wrong?"

"I hit my head on the window." She chuckled. Trying to use humor as a way to cover the pain. "Do you have class today?"

"Not today. I only come twice a week."

"Okay. Well, I guess I'd see you later on."

"Yeah. I'll hit you up."

As she watched him pull away. Jasmine took a deep breath and slowly started her walk up the breezeway. A chill came over her as the wind continuously blew. Which caused her teeth to chatter because she didn't think to grab a jacket. Although, she loved the fall. Jasmine hated when the weather neared winter.

Walking into the class. Jasmine got over joyed when she saw shelly waving at her. When they met the previous day, neither of them asked one another what classes they had enrolled in.

"Girl…. Mario put it down last night." Getting excited again from the thought of her encounter the night before.

"What!" Stunned by the news. "You just met him yesterday!" Slapping her hand on the desk. *This bitch is crazy. I can see that already.*

"I know. It kind of just happened I guess." Feeling ashamed now that she actually heard it out loud. But, distracted by the heat she suddenly felt between her thighs.

"It kind of just happened!" *I know she didn't just say that.* "How does something like that, kind of just happen?" Shelly said. *I need her to break this down to me because I'm beginning to feel a bit remedial about this whole situation right now. This is too much stress for me to even deal.*

"I don't know. But, it did." Dismissing the conversation.

(Beep, beep) Jasmine phone alerts.

"I think it's him!" Blurting to Shelly enthusiastically.

"Girl, he just sent me a text!" Astonished, because she wasn't expecting to hear from him so soon.

"Already!" Surprised because she assumed Mario to have been the hit it and quit it type of guy. *Damn… She must've really made it worth his time then.*

"Yeah." Grinning like a Cheshire cat.

"Well, what it say?" Anxious to hear the juice.

Mario: Hey baby, I miss you and my kitty. Can't wait to taste you later on this evening.

"He called me Bay Be!"

"Yeah, I guess." *That's all he had to say…* "So does this mean y'all a couple now?" Raising her brow. Staring blankly at Jasmine, awaiting an answer.

"Duh!" Slamming both her hands down on the desk.

"I was just asking, calm down. Geesh…."

"And I was just answering."

"Well good luck with that."

"Don't be jelly."

"Jealous of what!" *I know this trick ain't just try me like that. What the hell I got to be jealous for. Definitely not over no quick dick.* "Don't do that." She advised.

"Cause he's mine. They may have wanted him once but I jump to the head of the line." She serenaded.

"Righhhhhtttt….." Agreeing sarcastically. *Of course you did. With pussy in his face. The other hoes the ones who should be worried.* Shelly cracked to herself.

Day after day, Jasmine and Mario would hook up after school to sex. But, neither of them ever stated they were an item officially. Since they've been carrying on for almost a year and a half now. In her mind they were together. But, through his eyes. Mario saw things a little differently.

"Who you on the phone with?" She questioned. Trying to figure, why he's not giving her any attention. Walking off, Mario continued to pay her no mind as if she wasn't talking to him at all. *I know he didn't just walk off on me.*

"I said! Who the heck you on the phone with, Man!"

"Hold on, hold on real quick. This bitch stepping out her lane." Responding to the individual on the other end of the receiver.

"Bitch!" Squeezing his cellular phone in his hand. "Didn't I tell you not to question me about who the fuck I'm talking to on my got damn phone!" Pointing it in her face.

"Hold the fuck up!" She interrupted.

"Shut the fuck up!" He bucked back at her. "I'm talking now!" He demanded. "Last time I checked, I pay this phone bill!" Jerking the phone back and forth in the air. "Ima call you back bay. Let me handle this situation real quick." He soothed. Catering to his lover on the other end of the line.

"BABY!" Approaching him. "Who the fuck is you calling baby!" As soon as Jasmine got the last part of 'baby' off her lip. Mario smacked her down in the floor.

"Bitch!" Gripping that word from the pit of his stomach. "I told you over and over about questioning me regarding my phone calls and my freaking where about! I go where I want and I talk to whomever the fuck I feel like bumping my gums with." He shouted. "You ain't my bitch! And you ain't my mother fucking mama! You maggot ass hoe!"

Consumed with disbelief. Jasmine remained on the floor holding her cheek. She still can't believe Mario hit her. In a years' time, she's noticed his anger issues. But, it never dawned on her at any point of him being abusive. One things for sure, her feelings was hurt. But, she can't blame no one but herself.

"You just a hoe I put up with to suck my dick!" He ranted. "Know

41

your place!" As he heads to the bathroom, Jasmine spots his phone sitting on the couch. "Swear you give these bitches the 'D'. They think they got rights to your ass." He said aloud.

As she watched him walk down the hall. Jasmine grabs it and immediately rushes out the door. Taking the stairs, she makes a call to see if one of her friends could come pick her up. Sticking around wasn't something she intended on doing. Once Mario finds out she took his phone. Things were definitely going to escalate from there. Standing on the edge of the sidewalk, Jasmine awaited Nichole's arrival. Every car that drove pass, made her even more nervous then she was in the beginning. Because she assumed it to be Mario. After about seven minutes, Nichole finally pulled along side her.

"Thanks for picking me up in such short notice." She thanked. Closing the passenger door as she leaned over to hug her dear friend.

"Oh, it's no problem boo." Opening her arms to greet Jasmine back. "I was in the neighborhood anyway." Letting her know it wasn't a inconvenience. "What's going on?" She asked innocently. Trying not to come off nosey.

"Mario and I had a disagreement and I really needed to get my stuff and go." Bowing her head as she confided in her friend. "What you doing out so late?" Looking up at Nichole. "Usually you'd be in the house around this time." Trying to manipulate Niko into spilling the beans about where she was coming from.

"Nothing major. Just riding around trying to clear my head." She sighed.

"Is everything okay?"

"Yeah, I'm good." She assures Jasmine. "Just one of those days, I guess." Keeping her eyes focused on the road.

"I know what you mean." Grabbing her bag from under the seat. "Trust me. I know exactly what you mean."

As they pulled closer to Jazz's complex. She reached down in her bag and pulled out ten dollars to pay Nichole for picking her up. She didn't believe in riding for free.

"What's this for?" She asked. Looking down at the money as Jasmine tried to hand it to her.

"So you can get yourself some gas."

"Okay. But, you know I wasn't going to charge you." Snatching the money out her hand. "Since you offered." Continuing to count. "Gas is kind of high for me to be turning it down." She joked.

"Thanks again, Niko."

"Don't mention it doll."

"I'll talk to you later, okay." Jasmine promised as she leaned over the passenger window.

"Sure thing, hun."

Twisting the key in the front door. Jasmine stepped in the foyer and gave a big sigh of relief. "I can't believe the night I've had." She said to herself. Feeling for the hall light switch. She dropped her bags at the door and made her way to the living room to make a phone call. While dialing, she contemplated on how she would explain her present situation to judgmental Shelly.

"Hello." A voice came through the receiver.

"Girl, I'm scared." Whispering as she held on to the phone like her life depended on it.

"Why?" Shelly question. Trying to act as if she was concerned. "What done happen now?"

"I was over Mario house."

Oh lawd.

"And I caught him on the phone talking to some girl again."

I knew this conversation had to do something with him.

"I started questioning him about who he was talking to and he got mad."

Of course, tell me something I don't know. She thought.

"So, why you calling me?" Rolling her eyes because she wasn't in the mood to listen to the Jasmine and Mario drama tonight.

"Because I needed someone to talk to and tell what's going on. Just in case something big went down." She explained. "I took his phone when he was in the bathroom." Clutching the receiver in the palm of her hand. Looking over her shoulders from paranoia. "I got all my stuff I had with me and had Niko come pick me up. But, she don't know the details of what's going on."

"Annnnndddd, this is relevant to me because." Looking down at her finger nails. Debating if she should clip them or not.

"If he comes over there looking for me. Tell him I'm not there."

What the hell! She always putting me in the mix of their shit! Swear I need some new friends. Startled by the thought of him coming to her place, starting shit with her.

"Of course you ain't here!" Getting roused. "Why would he think that?" Restraining herself from hanging up in her face.

"Because he might think I came over there." Debating with Shelly. "That's why!" She yelled. Because she felt Shelly was attempting to make the situation appear smaller than it actually was.

"Hold on, let me look out the window real quick."

As Jasmine waited on Shelly to check to see if Mario was outside. She bit down on her nails. Never in a million years. Did she ever think, she would be victimized in this way. Especially, not by the man she loved.

"Girl!" Shelly screamed. "He outside my house!" Shouting in the phone. Feeling a sharp pain shoot threw her heart after hearing the fear in Shelly's voice. Jasmine body started shaking uncontrollably.

"For real?" Hoping Shelly was playing a joke on her.

"Yeah, for real!" Appalled at the assumption of her being dishonest. "What you think this is a game?" In defense mode. "Trick I don't do this shit for fun!" She argued. "What am I supposed to do?" Anticipating Jasmine's next words to guide her on what to do next. Before a response could be given, Jasmine heard the doorbell ring in Shelly's background. From that point on, all she heard was Mario and Shelly fussing.

"Girl!" Directing her attention back to Jasmine. "You better give this man back his cell phone!" She demanded.

"He ain't gon' shoot you."

"I can't tell!" Shelly screamed. Staring down the barrel that was pointed in her face.

"That's a water gun." She responded jokingly.

"It looks real to me!" Frustrated, because Jasmine wasn't taking Mario's threats seriously. "You better stop playing with this man and give him back his shit! Cause ain't nobody got time for this!"

"Put him on the phone." She asked. Trying to remain as calm as possible to give an impression that she had the situation under control.

Placing the phone in Mario's hand, made Shelly feel a bit of relief. She had faith that things would be smoothed out from this point on.

"BITCH!" Mario screamed. Which caused Shelly to become nervous, because she assumed things would get better now that they're talking. But, assumptions get you nowhere. "You better give me my shit before I shoot your friend!"

Shoot who?

45

"And I don't bullshit." Shelly's heart sank. She knew Mario was serious about pulling the trigger. But, she couldn't understand how Jasmine was willing to test the waters with her life at stake.

"Whoa, whoa, whoa." Throwing her arms in the air. "All this ain't even necessary." She butted in. "I ain't got nothing to do with this right here." Attempting to reason with him. Staying as calm as possible, so she wouldn't trigger any switches that would cause things to escalate more.

"Nigga! You ain't gon' do shit but cause a scene and her mama gon' call the police on yo stupid ass! And get you locked up for trespassing and attempted murder." She mocked.

"Try me BITCH!" He roared.

As Shelly watched how Mario's shoulders arched back and chest swelled up. It didn't take but a second for her to cunningly ease her body back into the doorway. In an attempt to hide behind it.

"I don't give a fuck! To be honest." He screamed. Pacing back and forth with the phone and gun in hand. "You got my shit!"

"This is between me and you!"

"I don't think this trick heard a thing I just said." Talking to himself. "Didn't I just say I don't give a fuck?"

"You see I ain't over there, so you need to leave her alone." Hoping to convince him to leave.

"First off Bitch. I feel I need to let you in on something. Cause it seems to me like something ain't clicking in that head of yours. To where you can understand what the fuck I've been saying to you for the last five minutes. I said, 'I don't give a fuck'. Which means; I don't give a fuck about nobody being scared of shit! You took something from me. Therefore, that means I take something from you. Kapish."

"Fuck you!"

"We'll see about that."

Walking in circles around the house. Jasmine didn't know what her next move should be. She amplified the situation between her and Mario, higher then what it originally was. Therefore, she knew nothing good would come from any of it. BOOM! BOOM! BOOM!

"Someone's knocking at the door." Nique shouts.

"Y'all go to the room and if anything happens call the police." She warned.

"Okay." Her cousins agreed. Just as soon as Jasmine opened the door. Mario stepped in and started choking her.

"Bitch!" He yelled. "I told you about fucking with my shit!" Unable to breath. Jasmine had a split moment where she forgot what to do next. "You ain't got no fucking respect!"

Since he caught her off guard. The only thing Jasmine thought to do that could potentially save her life was to pull on his dreads. The more she pulled, the looser his grip became around her neck. It didn't take long for them to start physically punching one another. After the brawl. Jasmine took his phone out of her pocket and launched it over the balcony.

"Stupid, bitch!" Mario yelled as he looked at her. Wanting to sock it to her once more.

"Ya, mama!"

Mario proceeded to make his exist because her little cousin threatened to call 911. Walking back in the house, Jasmine almost broke down in tears. Wanting to let it all out, she refused. She felt she wouldn't give him the satisfaction. With all the adrenaline she had left, she needed to clear her head and vent a little more. Reaching for her cellular phone. Her fingers went to work.

Shelly knew who it was, but, she wasn't sure if she wanted to pick up.

After everything that went down, she'd had enough of the Jasmine and Mario drama for one night. As the phone continued to ring. She went ahead and answered it, because she knew Jasmine would call back until she got a response.

"Girl…." Is all Shelly could hear, before she even greeted her hello. "He came over here and we started fighting." She exclaimed. "Nique was crying and she threatened to call the police on him if he didn't leave." Getting more excited as she relived the events.

"Say what…."

"Girl, yes. That's the only reason he left."

"That ass didn't want to go to jail, I see." Shelly laughed as she tuned in to the late night gossip, she couldn't wait to hear more of.

"I broke his phone and I told you that was a water gun."

"You did what… And what happened after that?" Holding on to the phone so she wouldn't miss not one word.

"Once again, Mario ain't gon' shoot no damn body girl."

"Just don't add me in y'all mess, next time y'all want to call y'all selves fighting."

"Bitch you were scared." Jasmine laughs.

"Hell yeah, I was scared! Water gun or not! He was pointing that junk in my face, not yours!"

"Whatever bitch."

"Don't whatever me. Your ass was scared to."

"Hell, yeah! When I opened that door, I knew my life was over."

"See, and you trying to talk big like you got balls of steel or something. Ho sit down."

"I know right. But I stuck with that ass."

I would hope so.

"If he didn't have those dreads he would've had me, but alright then honey. I'll call you tomorrow.

"Alright then."

"Good night."

"Good night, crazy."

AN UNEXPECTED GUEST

"Just one more push and we can finally meet your baby girl." The doctor tells the expecting mother.

"Uhh!" She grunts.

You could hear the voice of a baby crying in the background. The whole room was completely silent, when the baby finally arrived. Being this was her first child. She didn't know what to expect, now that the baby was actually here.

"She is so beautiful." He said. Slinging the baby to the nearest nurse, so she could clean her as quickly as possible.

"Mama, I'm not ready to be a mother yet. I still have things I want to do with my life right now and I know keeping this baby will stop everything I want to do."

"Well, what are you looking for me to say?"

Looking over at her mother, then down at her hands. Unsure of what her mother would say about the decision she's prepared to make. She sighed. Thinking to herself, how could she be so selfish to someone who doesn't deserve this. But, she knew within herself. This was something she wasn't ready for.

"I'm not giving up my only grandchild, if that's something you were trying to consider." Telling her daughter forcefully so she would have a clear understanding of the message she was giving.

"That's not an option. So you can scratch that thought."

"Could you please take on the responsibility for me as if you were her mom?" She begged. "If you signed the birth certificate, then we both can get what we want." Trying to turn this deal into a sure transaction. "I can promise you I'd make sure to make something of myself to provide for her. Therefore, no stress will be on you. But she can never find out under any circumstances that I'm her mother." Looking down at the baby as she slept in her arms.

"I'll keep this secret. But if you fail to uphold your end of the bargain, I will put you out of my house. And, prepare yourself to be served child support papers."

"I understand." Leaning down to kiss the baby on the cheek as she gave her one last hug as her mother.

SHELLY

Buzz, buzz, buzz. The alarm clock sounds. "Shut up!" Shelly screams. Leaning over to smack the snooze button. "It's 6:30 a.m already!" She grunted. "Uggh!" Still lying in the bed. "Man, I don't feel like getting up." Playing foot-sey with her feet. Trying to re-heat them under the covers. 'Today's my first day at Silverman and I'm already late'. She thought. Emerging from the bed. Shelly dragged her feet slowly. She bumped into the dresser and tripped over a pair of shoes she had laying in the floor. As she made her way to the bathroom, she then reached for her hair iron. But, noticed it wasn't where she placed it the night before.

"Candice!" She yelled down the hall. Regretting to consider everyone else was still asleep. "Do you have my Beverly Iron!" Peering out the door.

"No!" Candice announces back. "Ask Nette!" Frustrated, because her sister woke her up from the best damn dream she'd had in weeks. The all you can eat buffet dreams don't come that often. "She may have it!" Tossing the covers back over her head to shield her eyes from the light, that was shining through her doorway. "Dag, that pork chop was juicy."

Storming down the hall, Shelly bursts into Antoinette's room. Rambling through Nette's personals she had scattered on the dresser. Shelly had a hunch she'd find it in the clutter.

"Durn, can you knock first." Her sister questioned sarcastically.

"Hand it over!"

"Girl gone! I don't even know what you're looking for."

"Where is it? I know you got it!" Shelly accused.

"If you don't get yo psycho butt out my room demanding shit. Ima tell mama you in here stealing." Laying completely still in her bed.

"So, tell her!" She urged. "It's mine anyway. You took it from me."

"Whatever bitch, just get out." She advised as she reached under the bed and hands Shelly the iron.

"Don't let the door knob hit ya, where the good Lord split ya." She mocked. Thrusting her body back in place.

"Bitch!" Yelling as she made a bee-line back to her room.

After getting dressed. Shelly didn't have enough time to make herself breakfast. Instead, she grabbed a bagel and headed for the door. "I'm gone." She yelled. Once again, having no respect for the sleepers. "I should be home around three!" Snatching her keys off the banister and slamming the door as she left.

Upon her arrival. Shelly admired the view of the freshly cut lawn. Watching the students walk across the street with back packs, made her feel like she was in high school all over again. But, the difference this time around she had a bit more freedom. After, finally finding a parking space. Shelly took one last look in the mirror to make sure her hair was still intact. *Can't be looking ratchet on the first day.* She thought. As she patted her bangs down to make sure they were neatly in place. Once she was satisfied, she got out. Making her way up to the doors of her new school. She noticed one of her old classmates standing by the water fountain.

"Niko, is that you?" Posing with her hands on her hips. Shocked to see a familiar face.

"Hey girl!" An excited Nichole greeted back, throwing her hands in the air, over joyed because she finally saw someone she'd recognized. "I didn't know you were coming to 'Silverman'." Squeezing the life out of Shelly.

"Yeah, girl." Trying to shake the awkwardness off. "It was close to home. Which meant I could still work, while I'm here."

"Okay… Sounds like a plan."

"You know I needs my money." Fanning her hand.

"I heard that." Agreeing with Shelly. For she knew what she meant about being able to hold a job while in school. "What's your major?" Wondering if they had similar interests.

"Fashion and Design. What's yours?"

"I decided to study Accounting." An unenthused Nichole said.

"That's what's up." Noticing the change in her friends tone.

"Where you headed?"

Looking down at her schedule. Shelly used her finger to guide her through the dates and times. Until she found what she was looking for.

"I got College Algebra with Dr. Greene right now." She said. Looking up at Nichole, hoping she'd say that's where she's going as well. "Where you headed?"

"I got English 1101 with Professor Reid."

"Oh, well let's meet up at eleven in the café and maybe we could hang or something." Shelly suggested.

"That's cool with me."

As Nichole walked away, Shelly walked into her class and took a seat towards the rear. Placing her back pack on the side of her desk. She leaned down to pull out her things and get herself prepped for her teachers arrival. Opening her book she glanced towards the door and noticed a Puerto Rican girl approaching her with a smile. Unsure of what she was smiling about. Shelly smiled back instinctively.

"Hey, my name is Jasmine. What's yours?" She greeted.

"What's up, my name is Shelly. Nice to meet you." Stretching her hand out to meet hers for a hand shake.

"Thanks, you to."

After taking a seat, Jasmine started unloading her books on to the desk and pulling off her jacket as well.

"Is this your first day or are you a returning student?" She leaned over to ask Shelly.

"Na, this my first day."

Damn she nosey. Shelly thought. Being she's not usually the friendly type. "How about yourself?" Asking because she didn't want to come off rude.

"This my first day as well. Hell I was almost late!" She joked.

"Me too." She chuckled.

"It's Shelly right?"

"Yeah." *Didn't I just tell her that.*

"Do you have your textbook yet?" Anticipating her response.

"Yeah, I got it last week." *I knew that was coming. It never fails.* Shelly thought. *Folks don't never come to school prepared. Soon she gon' be asking to borrow a pen. Then a scan-tron, then some paper, and then my cell phone.*

"Do you mind if I share with you today? I have to wait after class to get mine."

"Sure, I don't see why not. I don't mind." Forcing a smile on her face. *Why she looking like that. I ain't gay bitch.*

"Thanks."

"No biggie."

As Jasmine continued to settle in, she looked up and saw the man she never thought existed.

'I wonder what our teacher is like'. Shelly thought.

"Damn, he fine!" Getting more excited as she leaned over and elbowed Shelly to direct her attention towards the door. *This bitch is crazy.*

"Girl, girl, girl, girl, girl." Rubbing her hands down her leg. "I got to have him on my team!" She stated. "Just wait, you're looking at my future right there." Boasting to Shelly.

Lost in the sauce, Shelly shook her head and smiled. 'I wonder if I'll have time to go drop my samples off today'. She thought as she gazed into space. 'Maybe I can convince Nichole to ride with me to 'Stylez'. I'll ask her when I see her'. When the instructor finally arrived. He didn't speak a word to the class. He came in, placed a roll sheet at the end of the table, and passed out the class syllabus.

"We will have our first quiz Thursday and will prepare for the first exam next Tuesday. Class is dismissed."

"Damn, that was fast." Shelly mumbled. "If I knew class was going to be like this, I wouldn't have rushed to get here the way that I did." She complained. "These teachers a trip." Shaking her head. "I tell you the truth." Walking towards the door, Shelly saw Jasmine talking to the guy she was drooling over during class. Once he'd walked away. She approached her.

"Damn girl! You moving a little fast ain't you?" Surprised because she underestimated Jasmines ambition to get what she wanted. "You ain't even been here two whole hours yet. Let alone seen what the rest of your classes looking like and you already all over this man." *Fast ass.* Cutting her with her eyes.

"When you know. You know girl." She advised. Googly eyed.
From that moment on, Jasmine and Shelly became inseparable.

"I still think you're crazy for doing that."

"You'll live." Fanning her hand at judgmental Shelly as she continued to watch Mario walk down the hall until she couldn't see him anymore.

Looking down at her watch, Shelly realized time was speeding by. She thought she was still on schedule for her afternoon meeting. But, time had caught up with her.

"Damn, it's almost eleven!" She shouted. "Fooling around with that darn girl about to have me late." Picking up her pace.

Walking across the field to make her way to the café. Shelly spots Nichole walking a few steps ahead of her.

"Hey!" She yelled. Sounding as alley as 'alley' can get.

Nichole turned around after hearing Shelly's voice. Finally catching up with her. Shelly bent down to catch her breath and rested her hands on her knees.

"Hey." She greeted. "I was trying to see if you wanted to ride with me to drop these samples off at the shop." Breathing extra hard as she looked up at Nichole a few times.

"Are you okay?" Concerned, because she could see Shelly was definitely out of shape.

"Yeah, I'll be fine. Soon as I catch my breath."

"Sure, I'll ride with you. I ain't got nothing else to do anyway." Shrugging her shoulders.

"Okay, it'll be fun."

"And maybe one day you can come with me to the gym. Cause you got needs girl." Laughing as she continued to watch Shelly struggle for air.

"Ha, haa. Real funny."

"No seriously. My trainer Keith, with KTX Fitness. Can get you right together honey, and he's economically priced."

"I may have to consider that. At least, when my schedule permits it."
"Deal."

Shelly had worked for 'Styles' since her senior year of high school. The owner had grown quite fawned of her and had taken her under her wing as a mentor. Because, Shelly has so much potential. Kelly decided it was time to reward her.

"Ms. Brown, we've been expecting you." Kelly greeted as she slid across the boutique floor.

Who is 'we'. Shelly wondered as a sharp pain throbbed in her heart. Nervous of what she have or hadn't done properly.

'Am I fired?' She questioned herself. 'I've been coming on time for the past two years, and have done everything this trick has ever asked of me to do. Now she sittin' around here trying to be all slick. If she fires me. I'm going to give her a big piece of my mind. Her clothes ain't all that anyway.'

"You have?"

"Yes dear. I have someone here I'd like for you to meet." Smiling as she led Shelly to her office.

As they walked passed the cash register. Shelly got more nervous then when she went to the doctor for her annual check up. Nothing pains her more then to not know something before it happens. She wasn't to thrilled about surprises. When Kelly reached for the door knob, Shelly could have fainted from the anxiety she was feeling. Before you knew it, she was standing in front of a man with a welcoming smile on his face.

"Mr. Jenkins, this is the young lady I've been constantly boasting to you about." Kelly introduced. Pushing Shelly from behind to meet the guy in a faded blue suit.

Shocked by her words. Shelly felt bad for what she intended on saying to Ms. Kelly, if she'd planned on letting her go.

"I really believe she has the potential we're looking for and the freshness this industry so desperately needs right now." Patting Shelly on the shoulder. "If nurtured by the right people. She could surely soar extremely high." She continued to boast. "And be a product I'm proud to say I've helped derive."

"Hello." Stating with a deep and masculine voice. "My name is Arnez Jenkins." Sticking his hand out to greet hers. "It's a pleasure to finally put a face to the name."

"Hi, I'm Shelly Brown." Blushing because she was overwhelmed with how attractive he was. "It's a pleasure to meet you as well." Stumbling over her words, as a result of being star stricken by his presence. Shelly tried to inch her hand away before he noticed her perspiration levels began heightening.

"Kelly has told me great things about you. And with all the accolades I've been receiving. I knew, it would be crazy of me not to come see what all the commotion was about." He said enthused.

"By chance, do you have any of the samples I've asked you to bring in with you today?" Kelly asked, trusting she didn't forget.

"Yes, I have them right here." Swinging her back pack off her shoulder.

"You have to excuse her excitement Mr. Jenkins." She chuckled. "I never revealed unto Shelly that you were going to be joining us today."

"What a surprise." He smiled as he awaited her to reveal the masterpiece that was hidden in the bag. "I guess that means she's not aware of my investment either, is she?"

'What the heck are they talking about?' Shelly thought. 'I know he's not saying what I think he's saying.' Getting even more nervous while she fumbled through the cloths.

"No, I kept that part a secret as well." Snickering as if someone had told her a secret and she was the only other person on the planet who knew.

When Shelly finally processed the news. She didn't know what to make of it all. Here stood 'Arnez Jenkins', a well renowned investor. Who'd just opened up a new club down on Yellow Ridge Rd. called 'The Spot'. And now he's actually standing in front of her inquiring about an investment in her designs. Never in a million years did she think she'd be standing here in this moment. She was in complete awe of the things that had begun unfolding before her hazel eyes and didn't know how to react to the news.

"Have you thought of a name for the actual product yet?" He asked.

"Not yet." She admits. Disappointed in herself for not being prepared for moments as this. "I can't seem to come up with anything catchy right now. Plus, I never thought I would have to make a decision so sudden."

"Since this is your baby and you're the creator. You have to name it." He advised. "But you can't think of it as just a name." Pausing because he started to feel the passion from his words as he spoke. "It's your 'brand'."

'Wow'….. Shelly thought. 'My brand'…. Staring into space with her mouth wide open. If a fly was buzzing around, this would be the perfect opportunity for it to seek shelter.

"Honestly, when I started creating my patterns. I never thought it would go as far as to getting the attention of an investor." Feeling ashamed of her own disbelief. "You dream of things like this. But, you never truly believe it will happen."

"When you're ambitious enough to step out and say 'I want to establish myself in this world'. You can never put a limit on your success." He told her. Finding more inspiration for himself through his own words.

"Doors are made to swing open." Kelly blurted.

"I know, but sometimes your surroundings can discourage your motivation. Especially, if you don't have anyone else that sees and believes in your vision with you."

"Not only do I understand, but I can relate to that one hundred times over. But if you doubt you. Then, who is left to believe in you?"

Baffled by his riddle, Shelly concentrated on a name. She thought and she thought. She even considered using her own name as an option. But, she still wasn't satisfied.

"Nothing comes to mind. It's almost like my mind had gone blank." She laughed.

"What you think about 'Shine'." Nichole suggests.

"Shine!"

"Yeah, Shine." She states joyous to the idea of helping a friend. "Because they'll 'shine' like a starra every time they put one of your pieces on." Trying to convince them to grasps her concept.

"I like it." Arnez yaps.

"Well, 'Shine' it is!" Shelly confirms. Never giving the idea a second thought.

After leaving 'Stylez'. Shelly dropped Nichole off at home. When she was alone, tears began to well in her eyes. Her first thought was to thank God for all he had done for her. It appeared that doors were starting to open in her favor and she didn't know what her next move should be. Wanting to celebrate her joy, Shelly contemplated where she could go. She wasn't in the mood to go to any bars. But, she knew she had to tell someone the good news.

Pulling into her mother's drive-way. Shelly jumped out of her vehicle. So excited she realized she forgot her purse in the truck and left the head lights on. "Dang!" She blurted. Aggravated because she had to unlock the car just to get it out. So anxious, the door flings wide open. Bursting in; Shelly checked behind it to make sure there wasn't any holes in the wall from the impact. Her mother would have a field day cursing her out if there was.

"Mama! Mama!" Is what Debra heard echoing down her hallway.

Unsure of which child it was. Knowing didn't matter one way or the other. She knew they'd better have a good reason to be trampling through her house in such a manner, because she didn't tolerate horse play.

"Who is that yelling in my house?"

"Ma!"

"What is it?" Getting angry at whoever it was rudely interrupting the season primer of her favorite show.

"I just got signed!" Jumping up and down in front of the television, blocking Debra's view.

"You just got what?" Realizing her daughters body wasn't transparent as she shifted side to side to see bits and pieces of the picture. "Girl, you better start making some since. Cause I'm on the verge of slapping the taste out your mouth for running through my house. Yelling, screaming, and carrying on like you done lost your mind." Jerking the remote in her hand. "I'll sign you alright." She promised. "Now, get out the way!"

"No mama." Shelly laughed as she started to explain before her mother would launch the remote in her direction. "Arnez Jenkins just signed me."

"Who?" Now curious enough to seek interest in what her daughter was trying to tell her.

"He invested in my clothes mama!" Overly enthused. Wanting her mother to feel the same joy that she was experiencing.

"Slow down baby!" Sliding to the edge of the sofa while she rested her elbows on her knees. "Who did what?" Swirling the remote in her hand.

"We a BRAND now!"

"Okay, I'm lost."

"We made it mama!" She exclaimed.

"What! A brand!" She screams. Reanalyzing Shelly's words to get a better understanding of what she was trying to say. "Are you saying we have a investor?" Jumping from the sofa.

"Yes, mama!" Dragging her words impatiently because she had been trying to tell her that for the last five minutes.

"Awe baby, I knew you could do it!" Embracing Shelly as she congratulated her. "I knew you could do it!" She continued as tears of joy fell from her glossy eyes. Squeezing so tightly, that Shelly could hardly breath.

"Mama." Shelly mumbled.

"I'm so proud of you dumpling." Still squeezing and twisting from left to right.

"Mama, I can't breath."

"Ahhh, sugar." Placing Shelly's feet back on the floor. "I didn't mean to hurt you pudd. I just got a little overwhelmed. I'm sorry baby."

"That's okay. I understand. But I'm about to head home now. I just wanted to come over and share the news with you. I know I could've called but it's better face to face."

"Well I'm happy you stopped by and I am so proud of you muffin. Make sure you be careful running those streets so late like this now. You hear?"

"I hear you mama."

"Alright now. Call me and let me know you made it safely." Debra advised as she walked Shelly to the door. Continuing to peek around the corner to make sure the commercials were still playing.

"I will." Shelly promised as she turned and hug her mother goodnight.

"Alright now." Rushing Shelly off.

Excited about her new investor. Shelly couldn't wait to start planning for her future with 'Shine'.

When Shelly walked into her home. She noticed the red light blinking on her Caller Id. Once she locked the door. She then went over to check who she could've missed a call from. Before she could scroll down the feed good enough. The phone started to ring. Tossing her purse on the counter top, she grabbed the cordless and flopped on the sofa.

"Girl, I'm scared." She whispered through the receiver. Holding on to the phone as if her life depended on it.

"Why, what done happen now?" Trying to sound as concerned as she could. Even though, she was faking it.

"I was over Mario house."

Oh lawd.

"And I caught him on the phone talking to some girl again."

I knew this conversation had to do something with him.

"I started questioning him about who he was talking to and he got mad."

Of course, tell me something I don't know. She thought.

"So, why you calling me?" Rolling her eyes because she wasn't in the mood to listen to the Jasmine and Mario drama tonight.

"Because I needed someone to talk to and tell what's going on. Just in case something big went down." She explained. Wishing she had a vehicle of her own so she could hide over Shelly's house. "I took his phone when he was in the bathroom and had Niko come pick me up. But she doesn't know the details of what was going on between me and him."

"Annnnndddd, this is relevant to me because." Looking down at her finger nails, debating if she should clip them or not.

"If he comes over there looking for me. Tell him I'm not there."

What the hell! Giving Jasmine her full attention. *She always putting me in the mix of their shit!* Furious because she's always playing the middle man, even if she doesn't volunteer for the position. *Swear I need some new friends.* Startled by the thought of him coming to her place starting some shit with her.

"Of course you ain't here!" Getting roused up from the mess Jasmine done stuck her in. "Why would he think that?" Restraining herself from hanging up in her face.

"Because he might think I came over there!" She yelled. Wondering why Shelly was acting so inconsiderate. "That's why!" Getting angry because she felt Shelly attempted to make the situation appear smaller than it really was. To Jasmine, she saw shelly as the safe haven. No matter what the situation. She knew Shelly could fix anything. Even though they hadn't been friends for to long. She just knew Shelly was the crisis solver.

"Hold on let me look out the window." As Shelly pulled back the curtains. She couldn't help but notice a car driving recklessly down the hill. Pulling directly in front of her drive-way.

"Girl!" Shelly shouted. "He outside my house!" Screaming into the phone.

Feeling a sharp pain shoot threw her heart after hearing the fear in Shelly's voice. Jasmines body started shaking uncontrollably. This was bad and there was nothing she could do about it.

"For real?" Hoping Shelly was playing a trick on her.

"Yeah, for real!" Appalled at the assumption of her being dishonest. "What you think this a game?" In defense mode. "Trick! I don't do this shit for fun!" She argued. "What am I supposed to do?" Expecting Jasmine's next words to guide her on what she should do.

Ding, dong. The doorbell rings, causing fear to over come Shelly. As she reached to open the side door. She proceeded to ask 'who is it'.

"Where that bitch at with my phone?" Mario answered. Ready to tare the door down if necessary.

"I don't know, but she ain't over here." Sticking her head out the door so he wouldn't have to yell any longer.

"Is that her?" He asks aggressively.

"Yeah." He reaches down in his pants and pulls out something black. Once it was in full view, he points it in Shelly's face.

"You better tell that bitch to give me my fucking phone before I shoot your gullible ass." Aiming his gun at her forehead.

"Girl!" Directing her attention back on Jasmine. "You better give this man his freaking phone!" Panicking in fear for her life.

"He ain't gon' shoot you."

"I can't tell!" Shelly screamed. Starring down the barrel that was pointing directly in her face.

"That's a water gun." She responded jokingly.

"It looks real to me!" Frustrated because Jasmine wasn't taking Mario's threats as serious as she needed to be. "You better stop playing with this man and give him back his shit! Cause ain't nobody got time for this right now!"

"Put him on the phone." She asked. Trying to remain as calm as possible. To give an impression that she had the situation under control.

Placing the phone in Mario's hand, made Shelly feel a bit of relief. She had faith that things would be smooth sailing from that point on.

"BITCH!" Mario screamed. Which caused Shelly to become more nervous, because she assumed things would get better. But, assumptions get you no where. "You better give me my shit before I shoot your friend!"

Shoot who?

"And I don't bullshit."

Shelly's heart sank. She knew Mario was serious about pulling the trigger. But, she couldn't understand how Jasmine was willing to test the waters with her life at stake. After meeting one another in class. Shelly would've never guessed Jasmine would become a nuisance the way she had.

"Whoa, whoa, whoa." Waving her arms in the air. "All that ain't even necessary." She butted in. "This y'all situation, not mine. I ain't got nothing to do with this." Attempting to reason with him. Staying as calm as possible, so she wouldn't trigger any switches that would cause things to escalate more.

After fussing with Jazz. Mario places the cell phone on Shelly's car and walked to his vehicle.

"This bitch got life fucked up!" She announces. "Always putting me in the mix of her drama!" Shaking her head. "My mama told me to stop messing with her, but naw 'that's my friend'. To hell with that!" Slamming the door. "This helpha a hazard! Should've seen the warning label when we first met!" Shelly argued. "Shit!"

After dealing with her uninvited guest. Shelly went and ran herself a nice warm bath. The day had unveiled a lot of surprises and she wanted to ease her mind and soak everything in. When she sat down in the blossom scented water. She exhaled in relief of total relaxation. As she merged the yellow bar of soap with her rag, she smiled with her eyes closed. Focused on the meeting she had earlier that day. Her dream of bringing her designs to life has finally become a reality and she couldn't believe the way her life cards are being played. She was dealt a crappy hand, but as fate may have it. She's coming out on top.

Looking at the phone as it rang. Shelly knew it could only be one person calling so late in the night. And honestly, she couldn't make up her mind if she wanted to answer it or not.

"Girl…." Is all she could hear before Jasmine even greeted her 'hello'. "He came over here and we started fighting." She exclaimed. "Nique was crying and she threatened to call the police on him if he didn't leave."

"Say what…." Shelly could hear her excitement threw the phone.

"Girl, yes. That's the only reason he left."

"That ass didn't want to go to jail, I see." Shelly laughed as she tuned into the late night gossip she couldn't wait to hear more of.

"I broke his phone, and I told you that was a water gun."

"You did what… And what happened after that?" Holding on to the phone so she wouldn't miss not one word.

"Once again, Mario ain't gon' shoot no damn body girl."

"Just don't add me in y'all mess next time y'all want to call y'all selves fighting."

"Bitch you were scared." Jasmine laughs.

"Hell yeah, I was scared! Water gun or not! He was pointing that junk in my face, not yours!"

"Whatever bitch."

"Don't whatever me. Yo ass was scared to."

"Hell, yeah! When I opened that door. I knew my life was over."

"See, and you trying to talk big like you got balls of steel or something. Ho sit down."

"I know right. But I stuck with that ass."

"I would hope so."

"If he didn't have those dreads he would've had me, but alright then honey. I'll call you tomorrow."

"Alright then."

"Good night."

"Good night, crazy." Hanging up the phone. "Ain't nobody got time for her mess. I need to go to sleep so I won't miss this meeting in the morning."

The following day, Shelly had arrangements to have lunch with Mr. Jenkins. They'd planned on discussing the future of 'Shine' and update one another on what's been going on since they'd last spoke. Excited but not wanting to appear childish. She practiced the entire dialog she thought they would have during her drive. When Shelly arrived at 'BIC'S'. She noticed Arnez's foreign parked in one of the spaces closest to the door. By this being her first time dinning at this particular eatery. It took her longer than she expected to find it on the strip. Walking in, she saw him standing to direct her attention in his direction. Since he had been watching the door. He saw her as she entered.

"Good afternoon." He greeted with a smile. Embracing her with a snug hug to follow.

"Good afternoon." Blushing as she tugged on her skirt. "I'm sorry for being late. I had a time trying to find this place."

"That's ok. I'm an early bird anyway. So a extra seven minutes wasn't that bad." Pulling her chair from underneath the table. "Do you like Chinese Food?"

"Yeah, I don't have a problem with it." She lied. "Is that what they serve here?"

"Yep, ma'am. The best place I've found in this area so far. And for the prices they charge, it better be desirable." He laughed. "But don't worry about the prices. You can have whatever appeals to you."

"Thank you."

"Of course." Skimming through the menu.

"Shine is doing extremely well." Diving directly in. "And lately, I've been considering dropping my classes." Giving Arnez direct eye contact. To see what his reaction would be. "Doing so, I could have more time to take meetings and be more hands on with the manufacturing." Hoping he would agree. "Every item we've marketed so far, has sold out in every store. We still have back orders that need to be filled and I need to be apart of making sure it gets done." She explained. "The right way."

"Really." Surprised by the news.

"Yes." Giving off a smile. For she was proud of herself and astonished by the work she had done. "The fall collection premieres in another two weeks, and I'm eager now more than ever to focus on the next step." Ignoring the waitress as she offered her a refill on her pop. "With time, I would like to expand. But, not here in this state. I want to branch off and open another store up north somewhere." Taking a bite of the mixed vegetables she had on her plate. "My plan is to have one location in all states and then branch off to other countries."

"Wow." Leaning back in his chair, because he was amazed by the sudden boost of sales. And by her ambition. "I have to say, I am impressed." Taking the napkin from his lap and using it to wipe his mouth. "I knew we were doing well, but I didn't expect numbers to be as high as they've been."

"I know what you mean." Shelly agreed. Taking a sip from her glass before she continued. "The only thing I can focus on right now is how bad I want my product to be global."

"It will happen." He assures her. Taking a sip from his glass as well. "When the time is right." Crossing his feet underneath the table. "But in the meantime. Why don't you and your friends come down to the club and celebrate this weekend." He urged.

Did he really just invite us to his club. She thought to herself. Trying as hard as she could to hold her excitement in.

"Every things on me, since I'm benefiting from this venture as well." Placing the napkin on the table. "When you get to the door." Standing up from his seat. "Tell Rock you're my guest, and he'd take care of you from there." Pushing the chair under the table as he looked around for their waiter.

"Alright." Standing to her feet while she adjusted her skirt once more. "Thanks again Mr. Jenkins." Shaking his hand. "I really do appreciate this."

Remaining humble as she thanked him.

"Call me Arnez." Bending to kiss the back of her hand. "There's no need to keep things formal."

Wow, we on first name basis.

"So I hope to see you and your friends this Saturday."

"Indeed you will." She agreed. "Have a nice evening!" Shouting as she watched him walk away.

"You too, and don't be so hard on yourself. Everything will turn out great. Wait and see." He promised.

"Wait and see."

KICKING THRILLS

At the break of dawn, he could hear the sizzle of oil cooking at 180 degrees in the frying pan echoing down the hall. The sweet aroma from the apple wood bacon tickled his nostrils as the scent flooded the air. Suddenly, a loud explosion sounded from the toaster as two slices of bread jumped out to escape the heat. As two eggs were being smashed against one another to simmer. Whoever was in the kitchen knew their way around those pots. Mixing cheese and butter in the bowl of grits. She remembered the final touch of love would come from a cold glass of freshly squeezed orange juice. After taking time to prepare this meal. She gracefully set his plate and made her way to the bedroom.

"Baby, wake up." She encouraged. Feeling as if she could conquer the world after the night she'd had. "I made breakfast." Walking over to the bed with a tray full of food in her hands. Carefully, looking down to focus on her steps to make sure the juice doesn't tilt over.

"Is that right?" He responds as he turns towards her. Re-tucking himself underneath the covers, since the room felt like he was sleeping in a deep freezer.

"Yes, that's right." Smiling flirtatiously. "Now get up and eat this food before it gets cold." Placing the orange juice on the night stand. "You know you need something on that stomach before you go in today."

"Are you going to feed me?" He asked. Acting as if he couldn't function without her tending to his every need.

"Of course I will." Easing her feet out of her house shoes to sit beside him.

One things for sure when it comes to these two. The chemistry between them was undeniable. Instant lust at its best at first sight. And from that point on, they couldn't let go. No matter the situation. No matter the circumstance. If there was an open opportunity, they made that effort to spend it together. Whether it was house calls. On break at work. In the movie theater. Believe me when I say public restrooms were not off limits when it came to the expression of their desire. At the park in broad day light. Even at her mothers birthday gathering. They took advantage and found pleasure in doing so.

"Whatever you want shugg. I'm here to service you and only you." Kissing him on the forehead as she snuggled next to him.

Mixing the grits with the eggs to stir some of the excess water off. She knew her food was another reason he stuck around the way that he did. Satisfied with what she'd done. She glanced over at him and started servicing.

"What would you like to taste first?" She asked seductively.

Scanning over the plate, he couldn't decide what he wanted to savor first. Everything was visually appealing to him, and knowing satisfaction would come from whatever he chose. He went with the brightest thing on the plate.

"Let me see what a few of those eggs hitting on this morning." Running his tongue across his lips and pointing his finger like a five year old.

"Eggs it is….."

As she proceeded to place them on the fork, she motioned for him to open his mouth. After the fork met its directed destination. She lifted her arm to make sure he got all the contents off.

"Umm.." He grunted. Biting down on the fork.

"Yummy" she serenaded back, aroused from his groaning. "How is it?"

"Moist." He teased. Intending for it to be sexual.

"I'm happy to hear that." Antsy from his gesture. No matter what he did, big or small. Everything and anything that involved him lit her fire.

"You know what you be trying to do to a youngin', don't act." Staring at her from the corner of his eye. Thinking of all the things he wanted to do to her if only he had the time. With all the things her main man wouldn't do serenading in the back of his mind.

"And what's that?" Unsure of what he meant.

"You know." He accused. Bobbing his head as he groped his jock.

"Are we still going to the Camions like you promised this weekend papa?" Quickly changing the subject as she placed the fork down on the plate.

"Yeah, I've already made arrangements to make that happen for us." Picking the fork up so he could finish where she left off.

"All I need you to do is show up." Stuffing his face with bacon. "Your flight leaves Friday. I won't arrive until early Saturday." Licking his fingers. "I arranged it this way because I have a few things I need to get squared away before I leave. And I would like for you to be settled in by the time I arrive." He continued. "I don't think it's fair for you to miss out on an evening of rest on my behalf." Continuing to chew. "Because when I get there 'rest' is not in the cards for you." He advised. "I need you rested."

Because he makes her nervous whenever she's in his presence, she knew she needed to follow his instructions precisely. This was going to be a weekend to remember and she was ready for whatever it had in store for her. But, little did he know. She had her own plans in store for him.

"Okay, pumpkin."

"And Renee!" Pulling her by the arm before she walked away.

"Talk to me daddy." Slightly turning her head, catching his eye in the act.

"Make sure you pack that piece I like seeing you wiggle out of."

The chill of his voice caused her stomach to bubble. I wouldn't call it butterflies. I think it was more like fear, because she knew he was about to dick her down in a way a man had never dicked her down before. And when it came to him. Satisfaction was guaranteed.

"Sure thing big daddy. Whatever you want." Twisting as she existed the room.

As Bernard dressed for practice. He overhead his phone buzz. Thumbing through the menu. He clicked on the message icon to see who it could be. **Shelly: Hey baby, I miss you. I wish we could've spent a little time together last night after dinner. Have a good day. Love you, just wanted to say good morning. Smooches.** After reading the message, he shoves it in his gym bag and heads for the door.

"I can't say that I'm torn between two women." He said to himself. "But I can say it's going to be hard choosing just one. If I don't have to, I won't."

Turning into the gym's parking lot. Bernard saw Michael's car parked in the main parking garage, so he pulled along side it. As he placed his vehicle in park. He contradicted himself whether or not he should respond to Shelly's text or leave it blank. He figured if he said nothing, he could use being at practice as an excuse on why he didn't respond. Technically it wouldn't be telling a lie because he was at practice, but at the time of the message he wasn't. Unloading his things, he heard someone shouting at him from a far.

"Hey man!" Michael yelled. Standing in the doorway.

"What's up!" He greeted back as he walked up the pavement.

"Nothing much, did you get enough sleep last night for practice brah?" Moving out the way so Bernard could step inside. "You know coach ain't taking no slack from us this week. Defiantly from the way we played the week before."

"Yeah, man." Acting nonchalant as he brushed past Michael.

"Dude! What was up with you last night?" Reminiscing on how strange Bernard was acting. "You had me worried about you man." Looking at him as if he could read his mind. "The way you were acting all suspicious and looking over your shoulder and junk. Had me like 'yo, B trippin'. What was up with that?"

"About last night." Pausing to figure out where he wanted to start. "Man, lately I've been having issues choosing between Shell and Re dog." Sighing because he predicted this was going to happen one day. But not this early in the game. He thought it would become a problem a year down the line.

"What you mean?" Concerned because he felt his decision shouldn't be optional.

"I mean, Shell is my heart and I love her to death."

"Right... Right..." Nodding in agreement.

"But, Renee fucks me better dude."

"Wow....." Eyes wide. Mouth open.

"It's getting real complicated around here." Rubbing his hand across his head.

"How so?"

"I never thought I would be in this mess as deep as I am, when I first started messing around with Re."

"I told you nothing good was going to come from this." Rubbing the hairs on his chin. "It never does brah. You know that."

"I know but she wears lingerie every time we sex. With the heels to match. Shoot...." Thinking on a previous encounter he and Renee had that night. Still rubbing his chin. "She know that ass be sittin' pretty in them shits." Stressing himself out about how hard it's going to be to lose one of his girls. "I think that's why she be putting that mess on."

"You think...." With sarcasm.

"Half the time, I don't even have to do nothing but lay there, and she'll do all the work yo."

"For real!"

"For real man."

"Dag, I need to get me one of them my dude." Dapping Bernard up.

"Renee a true freak dog. She moans, talk nasty to me, and she suck a mean dick brah. She make a nigga bitch up every time she do that shit too brah." Tapping Michael on the shoulder. "She got that onion honestly from her mama."

"Oooo weeeee....." He clowned. "That ain't something I'd tell people though." He chuckles as he continues to listen to his friend pour his heart out.

"And Shelly....." Scratching his head as he tries to decipher between the good and bad things he could say about his lady. "Shelly never wears sexy bedtime undies." Mike hunches over laughing hysterically. "She be having on granny panties and shit." Frowning in disgust. "I don't know if it's from her being with me as long as she has. To where she feels comfortable and she thinks she doesn't have to go that extra mile anymore. But it matters. Dog, it matters straight up."

"Really...." In shock of the image of Shelly being so beautiful but in granny panties. Just the thought turned him off. "I feel for you brah."

"I wouldn't have a problem with them if she had a variety of colors to choose from."

"A variety!" Yelling out humorously. "You know you ain't right for that. You ain't even right."

"Every time we go to bed. She put the white ones on. I mean, don't get me wrong. She do have several that's pink colored. But, she could invest in the ones with the patterns or something. Just to spice it up for a nigga, you know." Shaking his head as he thought more about the satin ones she wears from time to time. "A nigga like options."

"You want options!" He laughed in agreement.

"Hell, surprise me every now and again."

"I feel you man."

As Bernard continued to concentrate on what his next move should be. He got frustrated, because it's obvious with whom his interest lies. But choosing a person because of a sexual attraction can be a iffy situation. And the saying goes 'the grass ain't always greener on the other side'. But if the sex ain't there. Can you really maintain a happy relationship without it? The grass maybe greener but the rent sure is higher. Especially dealing with Renee. The difference between the two: Shelly works and has a good head on her shoulders. She may suck in bed, but she does bring a lot to the table. On the other hand Renee doesn't have a job and she shops like money is going out of style. But her good out weighs her bad. With sex being her good and that's something Bernard wasn't willing to compromise at this point in his life. He felt he could handle a few stores here and there. But will it be enough? Will Renee stay when the times get tough and the well runs dry? Could she hold her own and maintain stability for the both of them the way he knew Shelly could? With all of his doubts, he didn't want to make the wrong choice. But, he will have to choose soon.

"She always got them freaking rollers in here head!" He complained. Looking over at Michael who was now choking on his spit from laughing so hard. Reassuring himself Bernard couldn't make things any more funnier then what he'd already done. It really is a shame how he was dogging the woman that stood the tests of time with him. Even though they met when Bernard was on his good foot. Shelly remained by his side even now when his career is starting to turn for the worst.

"If only you knew." Michael uttered.

"Don't get me wrong the sex is great. But she ain't no 'Re'!" Confiding in his friend. Wishing for some type of understanding. "She really need to start giving that something extra like she was doing when we first hooked up." Thinking of giving her an ultimatum. "You feel where I'm coming from. Can't you?" Staring at a watery eyed Michael. Awaiting his input on the situation. Expecting some type of expert advice he could actually use.

"Yeah." He agreed. Clearing his throat. "I feel you." Using his sweater to wipe the tears from his eyes. "I've been in the position you're in once or twice in my lifetime." He admitted as he continued to clean his face. "Can't quit remember how many, but I've been there." Surprised by his friends confession. But he owned up to his mistakes as well. "Shelly is a good woman brah."

"True…"

"She got a lot going for herself."

"I know."

"She got her own whip. Got her own crib. No kids. Want kids. And, she got her own business dude."

"You do have a point…." Using his fingers to count all the positives Shelly has to offer and brings to the table on her own.

"It don't get no better than that!" *I don't understand these fools nowadays. But, who am I to judge.* "So what, she don't do everything Re do." Shaking his head side to side as he tossed his sweater over his shoulder. "Hell, Re a ho! Of course she trying to fuck your head up." *Duhh....* "She already know what her end game is."

"What's that?" Dumbfounded to the obvious.

"Cashing your check every month!" Staring at Bernard with a serious look on his face. "Niggas start acting concerned when you start mentioning his money. Don't play stupid on me now folk." Staring to feel sympathy for his friend. "Have you even tried discussing your issues with Shell?" Trying to give him the benefit of the doubt. Thinking this wasn't just guy talk. Maybe he discussed it with her and she still hadn't made the changes yet.

"No. But, this is something she should know automatically. Men like to be tempted. At least I can speak for myself concerning the matter. Tease me sometimes!"

He just want what he can't have. Any opportunity where a man can have his cake and ice cream and not have any repercussions ain't turning that plate down. I know I couldn't. Therefore I know he ain't.

"When I wake up in the morning. I want to be like 'damn'. I wake up to this every day and proud to fall asleep next to it every night. Not scared and limp!" He whined.

"Dude you wild'n."

"But you right."

"I know."

"This ain't even the main reason I've been on edge though….."

"What's really good then B?"

Unprepared for the bombshell that was coming his way. Michael leans up against the wall and folds his arms nonchalantly. Pacing the floor. Bernard was unsure of how he was going to deliver this news. Would he be judgmental or will Mike have sympathy for him. But, for the sake of his own sanity. It was imperative that he got it off his chest.

"She pregnant." Exhaling as the words eased off his lips.

"Who pregnant?" Uncertain if he was really ready for Bernard to answer that question.

Taking a deep breath and then sighing. Bernard hung his head and spilled the beans.

"Word!" Eyes wide. Eyebrows raised. Jaw hanging low. "Damn man! What you gon' do?" Knowing this was surely the end of his friends relationship. "Have you figured out how you were going to tell her?"

"What you mean?" *I know his simple ass didn't just ask me that.* "My plan is to keep hiding the shit!" Walking away to avoid any other questions Michael may try probe him with. "You're tripping!"

"I'm just saying. It got to come out somehow." Following him on the court. "How far along is she?"

"Three months."

"Damn…. You've been keeping this mess quiet for three months my nigga!" Amazed at how well Bernard can keep a secret. "I'm going to keep it real with you man." Retrieving the ball from the court side rack. "The plan is to kick it like I don't know what's going on, if she comes around asking me questions about it." Shrugging his shoulders. "Straight up."

"I understand."

"She keeping it?"

"Yeah, she claims she in love and wants us to be a family."

"That's expected."

"But you know she in it for the money." Taking a shot from the free throw line.

"It's a meal ticket! Duh… She ain't passing that shit up!" *I could've told him that.*

"That's fucked up though."

"Just let it play out and hope for the best."

"Nothing good ever comes out of stuff like this. All I can do right now is cross my fingers and hope when Shelly do find out. She stay down with a nigga. I do still love her you know."

"True. But, you know I ain't going to sugar code nothing with you. It's going to take a real miracle for that girl to stay down after this."

"And that's what I'm counting on."

Popping out of bed, Shelly reached over to check her phone for any missed messages. For she was confident she'd have some form of contact from Bernard that morning. "I know he at practice. But, he could've at least text back good morning or something." She complained. Contemplating whether she should cook breakfast or wait until she picks her sister up. Since she laid her clothes out the night before, the only thing Shelly had to do was brush her teeth and wash her face. "Let me go, before we end up being late for this appointment. I know it's going to be a hassle trying to pry that phone out this child hands anyway." Deciding not to prolong the time. Shelly grabbed her keys off the mantel and proceeded to locked up. When she arrived at her mother's house. Since they were off schedule already, she went ahead and decided to stay in the truck. BEEP! BEEP! Honking the horn impatiently. BEEP! BEEEEEEP!

"I'm coming!" Candice screamed. "Bay, let me call you back." Angry because her sister didn't call to let her know she was on the way. "Shelly out there honking like she done lost her dag blame mind!" Yelling into the receiver as she rushed to gather her things. BEEP! BEEEEEEEPP! "I love you too."

As Candice hangs up. She snatches her purse and heads for the door.

83

RING, RING, RING! The telephone rings, but she ignored it and slams the door.

"You always rushing some darn body!" She fused as she climbed into the big body.

"Maybe you wouldn't feel so rushed if you weren't always on that dag blame phone!" Watching Candice struggle to climb in the seat. She was only about a good five feet and two inches.

"I was talking to my boo!" Buckling her seat belt. "A little something you need to learn how to do from time to time…."

"Well you need to tell your 'boo' to buy you a cell phone then. So y'all can talk for as long as you want."

"Whatever bitch."

"Don't get sensitive now!"

"You got it." Throwing in the towel because she knew this was going to be a dispute she wasn't going to win. Especially, with it involving the use of a telephone.

"You're damn skippy…."

"Long as I got my beeper. I don't need nothing else. If I were to invest in a cell phone, mama would be calling me all times of the day. Questioning my where about and I don't have the time or the patience for all that. Keep tabs on yourself, not on me."

"It ain't about keeping tabs Candice. It's about being able to get in contact with you for whatever reason that may come up. But, I'm not going there with you because I know it's going to be a waste of my breath. You don't listen to nobody when they're trying to give your stubborn butt advice."

"Because every time y'all say something and we don't do it the exact way y'all think it should be done. Everybody want to have an attitude and I feel I'm grown and y'all need to let me make my own decisions and my own mistakes."

"And when we do and things don't go your way. Who you come crying to? Exactly, and I know you getting tired of me saying I told you so. Some days I enjoy being right. But, I don't want to be right all the time. I want to see you succeed. Not stumble every opportunity that comes your way. All I'm suggesting is that you consider some of the advice we give. You don't have to take it, just consider it."

"I hear you. But, I'm still not getting a cell phone Shell."

"Fine." Dismissing the conversation as she pulled in the vacant parking space.

Signing in on the guest registration book. The masseuse greeted the ladies before they had an opportunity to finish. Since he had been awaiting their arrival for quite some time. As they followed him down the hall to a dark room. Shelly reached deep in her purse to check her phone once more for any missed messages. But to her surprise, still no contact from Bernard. "Not one single missed call." She said to herself. Contemplating whether or not she should put her phone on vibrate. Knowing if she did, that would be the time he'd call. But, with her luck. He wouldn't. "I really need to reconsider this relationship." She admitted as she hung her head in disappointment. After the masseuse directed them to their designated areas. The girls undressed and stretched out on top of the two cold cushion filled tables. Making herself comfortable. Candice struck a conversation to lighten up the mood, sensing something was off with Shelly.

"I'm grateful you decided to take a day off for pampering, because I really needed this. Especially the massage." Talking to her sister as she used her eyes to investigate where Shelly placed her phone. "I know I got a lot of tension in these muscles baby." Wiggling her arms loosely on the sides of the table.

"I know." Shelly agreed. Resting her head in the soft hole carved into her table. "I felt I needed to get away and breathe for a bit. Even if it is only for an hour." Wanting to tell her sister everything that's been going on with her and Bernard. Just to confess her insecurities and have a different opinion on what she should do. 'I want to ask her advice'. She thought. 'But I don't need her judgment right now'. She sighs. The phone rings, but, neither of them acknowledges it. "Tell me why, when we were at 'BIC'S' last night. Jasmine was all over Arnez like she ain't never had a man in her entire life before."

"I bet they went back to the house and did it." Candice joked.

"I'm sure they did, knowing her." Slick jealous because she wanted that type of attention from Bernard. "I still can't believe they hooked up." Surprised because she knew this couple had the potential of being the perfect match. But, still puzzled about how they linked up. "I wonder how long they've been talking." Trying to think back on any possible hints Jasmine could've thrown that would've suggested signs of her being involved with someone. "Let alone, who made the first move." Crunching her toes together to relieve the tension from her knuckles. "It couldn't have been Jazz though." She pondered. "I know that for a fact."

"I wouldn't be so quick to jump to any conclusions, because she did make the first move on Mario."

"Yeah….. But, ever since then she hadn't approached anyone else. She said she was afraid of picking the wrong guy again. And we all know." Over exaggerating her statement. "Don't none of us want another Mr. Wright amongst the group."

"That's why I said he had to have been the one who asked her."

"I see your point." Shelly agreed. "After we get our nails done. Let's ride down to the boutique for a minute." She suggested. "I could surely use an extra set of hands while they're available."

"Use my hands for what?" Giving Shelly the evilest eye she could create. 'She think she slick'. Mumbling under her breath. 'Always trying to wine and dine somebody into doing something for her as pay back'.

"Just to help me change the store around a bit." *She better say yeah. She really don't have a choice in the matter because I'm driving anyway.* Snickering under her breath.

"I knew it was a catch to you asking me to hang with you today!" Getting aggravated with Shelly's conniving antics. "I should've said no!" Crossing her arms while she threw her tantrum. "You never do anything nice just for the heck of it." Lifting her body from the table. "You're always trying to milk some damn body."

As Shelly laughed at her sister remarks. She thought of how she always cleverly convinced people to do things for her and it made her laugh even more. She do have a tendency of being nice sometimes, but majority of the time it's for the favor.

"Tick for tat my sweet." She laughs. "You got to give a little to get a little." Finding humor at Candice's expense.

"I guess." Reaching for her robe.

While putting her clothes on. Shelly checked her cell to see who she'd missed a call from. "It better had been Bernard." Chanting arrogantly. Yet, wanting it to had been him. "I ain't heard from him all day." Getting antsy as she pulled it from her purse. Scrolling through the call log. Shelly noticed she'd missed three calls. But, none of them were from Mr. Anderson. They were all from the same unknown number with two voicemails to boot.

"Mama beeped me." Candice advised. "The message read urgent."

"I have a few missed calls myself, but I don't recognize the number." Trying to think back if she'd ever seen this number before. "You call mama, while I check my voicemails."

You have two unheard voice messages. To hear your first message. Please press one now. (Beep). Hello Ms. Brown. My name is Dr. Peterson and I'm calling in regards to your sister Antoinette. I'm sorry I have to inform you in this manner. But, Ms. Brown is in a critical state and I have been trying as often as I can to reach the closest family member to her as possible. I've tried your mother's home phone but I received no answer. This is the only other emergency contact she had listed on her medical chart. If you receive this message before I can attempt to contact you once more. You can find her here at Greenstone Hospital. Thank you and I hope to reach you soon. To return the message senders call please press five now. If not, press three to skip to your next message.

As confusion began consuming Shelly. She looked over at Candice and noticed her crying hysterically, while holding the phone provided in the room.

"What's wrong?"

"That was mama trying to call us."

"What she wanted?" Trying to remain calm after receiving the news.

"She said Nette in the hospital."

"I got a message from the doctor, but he didn't go into detail of what's going on. What she say happened?" Trying to control the ease in her voice, so she wouldn't alarm Candice of her fear.

"She said Nette was in a car accident and they had to rush her to the ICU. She's in critical condition Shell." Wiping the snot from her nose. "Gabriel was pronounced dead on the scene." She cried.

As tears welled in Shelly's eyes. She took a deep breath. Attempting to suck up every ounce of emotion she had that was unstable and took action.

"Let's go."

Speeding down I-125. Shelly tried not to lose control of the wheel. Going well over one hundred miles per hour. They were lucky the police weren't around at that time. Which was odd, because the state patrol usually stalk this particular freeway this time of day. Upon arrival, Shelly didn't think anything of parking. The first open space she saw was hers. And parking correctly wasn't a priority either. Her main focus was to get in that building by any means necessary.

"Good evening. How may I assist you?" The nursing assistant asked as they drew closer to the desk.

"Yes, could you point me in the direction of the trauma center please?"

"Right down that hallway and make a left. You can't miss it."

"Thank you." Shelly thanked with gratitude.

"No problem." The nurse smiled as she pointed them in the direction they were to go.

"Come on."

Walking into the waiting room. The girls saw their mother sitting in the middle of the sofa rocking her body back and forth. As they walked over to her, she stood and embraced them both.

"What happened?" Candice questioned as she sat next to her grieving mother.

"Apparently, last night Nette and Gabriel went to some fraternity party and had some drinks. Instead of riding with some of her other friends. Nette got in the car with Gabby and they had a collision with a tow truck."

"Fraternity party! Is she going to be okay?" Shelly asked. Trying to be the strong one out the group.

"I'm not sure." Sliding her right hand down her face. "No one has come and said a peep to me. I'm still waiting on the doctor to come and introduce himself and let me know more of what the hell is going on with my child." Gazing down the hall. Hoping to see someone come around the corner. "Lord knows I hope everything turns out okay."

"I knew something wasn't right, because Nette didn't call me back last night when they were leaving." Candy implied dramatically. "And it's not like Nette to not call. I can't believe this is happening." Shacking her head continuously as she cried. "She know better than this! I can't believe it."

Shortly after their intimate discussion. A tall Caucasian gentleman greets them as he enters the room. You could tell he was the doctor from the stethoscope he had laced around his neck. Nurses wear them, but they don't have the long coats on. Because of the length, Shelly felt comfort instantly.

"Good evening ladies." Smiling as he entered. "My name is Dr. Peterson and I am the physician that will be overseeing Antoinette's medical procedure while she's in our care."

"Procedure!" Candice wells.

"Give it to us straight doc." Debra stated as she arose from her seat. "Is my baby going to be alright?"

"Well, right now Antoinette is stable. But she needs a blood transfusion. Because of the amount of blood she's lost from the accident and from the transport to this location. We find it extremely important for us to move on this procedure as quickly as possible. In fact with the amount she is continuing to lose as her heart pushes the remaining blood. I'm afraid if we don't move on this swiftly. We will lose her within the next couple hours."

"Well, what is it that you're needing for us to do?"

"Being we're in the crucial stages. I need you ladies to go through a small procedure and then I can tell you where we go from that point on."

"What's first?" Shelly asked alert and ready.

"First, I need to take a few blood samples from the three of you to determine if either of you could be a possible match. And if one of you fits the donor qualifications. We can move forward from there." Reassuring the ladies. "My nurse will be in shortly to prep you. After the procedure is complete, I should have your results within minutes. Then we carry on." He instructed. "Everything will be fine. I can assure you Antoinette is in good hands." Smiling as he exited the room.

"Thank you, doctor!" Debra yelled. "He seemed real nice and personable."

"Yeah, he was charming."

"Now is not the time to be talking about how charming the doctor is or isn't. Antoinette is in there laying on her death bed possibly and y'all out here kicking thrills!"

"Candice you just need to shut up!" Shelly demanded. "Don't you think we know that! Maybe we're trying to see the better side of this mountain and think positive. Mama don't need to be stressing about something that's not going to happen. And Antoinette dying is not going to happen."

"I don't think his looks should be any of our concern right now."

"Stop arguing over nonsense! Candice you shut up and Shelly you go and try to find that nurse!"

"He said she'd be in here shortly."

"Well y'all shut up until she gets here then."

After about two minutes the nurse came in and asked them to follow her one at a time to draw their labs. Debra went first and then Candice followed next. Once they had finished the nurse asked them to sit in the waiting area until Dr. Peterson returned.

Patiently waiting in the waiting area. One thing consistently played over and over on Shelly's brain. 'Nette recovering by any means'. And any means truly meant by 'any means'. She started praying silently to herself for the Lord to step in and take control of the situation. Since the television was on, they could see the news reporter giving a live description of the accident as they watched. The camera crews from different networks all competed for the story aggressively. Not knowing the details or the extent of the accident until now. All three of the Brown ladies had front row seats to the viewing of what should have been a fatality.

"Excuse me ladies." Dr. Peterson interrupted.

"About damn time!"

"I have some good but also confusing news. First off I'm happy to inform you that Shelly's lab results came back positive for the best candidate for the procedure. But the thing that raised a brow of mine is her results also revealed Ms. Brown being Antoinette's biological mother." You could hear ants talking in the background. That's how quiet the room got. "I ran the test twice to make sure I didn't confuse the names on the tube, but it appears I did not have them mistaken." Candice looked over at her mother, then at Shelly. "Is this a correct paternity? Because if I am mistaken. We can run the examination again and be certain not to care for the samples in the same area."

"Yes it is." Shelly agreed. "How do we proceed with this?"

"If you could just come with me. My nurse will have you prepped and escort you to your room."

As Shelly followed Dr. Peterson. She could see the look of surprise on her sisters face. She knew one day this secret would come out. But, she still wasn't ready to face her demons just yet.

Left alone to wait for the next update. Candice started at her mother. She wanted answers and she wanted them now. Stunned that they've kept a secret as such from them for so long. She still couldn't digest Antoinette being her niece and not the sister she was raised to believe.

"Is it true? Is Antoinette really Shelly's daughter?"

"Isn't that what you heard?" Rubbing her head for she felt a headache on the horizon.

"Why did you lie?"

"It's none of your business why we did what we did!"

"Why have you raised us to believe we were all sisters?" Incessantly, questioning Debra. Trying to differentiate whether its anger or hurt she's feeling.

"This is not the time or the place for us to be having this conversation right now Candice."

"But I need to know mama!'

"Right now is not the time child!''

"Am I your child?" Feeling unsure of her paternity. Even though Shelly wasn't old enough to be her mother. If they could lie about something as big as this. Anything was possible.

"Stop this none sense! You know you're my daughter!''

"Antoinette not." Candice continued. "Who knows, y'all could've adopted me. Or maybe even have found me in a sewer some where. Honestly, I don't know what to believe anymore. I've always felt I didn't fit in and I don't look like either of y'all. All of you are fair skinned. Even daddy. I'm the only dark one." Rambling as tears fell from her cheeks. "You would assume the same if you were in my shoes."

"When Shelly had Nette. She was way too young to raise a child. So I kept her and we raised her as my child. That was the only other option we had." Never turning to look her in the face. "Shelly already planned on giving her up for adoption. No matter what I said, she wasn't changing her mind. I don't care what the circumstances are. Putting my only grandchild in government hands to give to some stranger to do with her whatever they may see fit; was not going to happen. Not while breath is still in my body and I am fully capable of making sane decisions. "

"Were you ever going to tell us?"

"Why should we? What need for either one of you to know? The way things were and the way you girls were raised together as sisters; as a family. As far as I'm concerned, Antoinette is my daughter. And that's final!"

"Are you going to tell Nette?"

"No! And I expect you to keep your mouth closed about it as well!" She demanded. "I don't want to hear anymore of this senseless talk from you ever again! You hear? This is the last time we will be having this conversation! And I do mean the last time! Don't make me have to repeat myself after tonight." She warned. Turning her back faced Candice as she placed her purse in her lap.

Candice didn't say another word. Still confused, she rested her elbows on her bag that was lying in her lap. As she tried her best to fix her face and think positive thoughts.

FOOLISH

Sitting at the table. Shelly started reminiscing on previous encounters she had with Bernard and took a sip as she continued to think. Because she wasn't a big alcohol drinker. The buzz kicked in immediately. The room felt warm to her and sweat had begun forming in her hands. Jasmine, trying to be as understanding as possible. Invited her over to relieve a pound of stress she was harboring on her shoulders. Therefore, both sat and sipped as they reflected on the past. Attempting to lighten the mood. Jasmine had an idea that she felt would make Shelly feel better. It's one thing for her to be down in a slump. But, to have her best friend in one with her. Was not a good look. Someone had to be happy and make the other feel their troubles were only a figment of their imagination.

"You want to call and invite Nard over for dinner?" Waiting on some type of emotional reaction from her friend. "I think it'll be cute for you guys to have some one on one time together." Stating with a little more enthusiasm. Trying to engage Shelly in conversation. "You know I can always go in the room to give y'all some privacy or go over to Michelle's house. You know she's just two doors down and that helpha always at home."

"Yeah…. That sounds nice." Slurring her words. Hiccupping after a loud burp sounded. "What do you have in mind?" Starring at her glass as she swung the contents around in a circular motion.

"Oh, nothing. Just a few crab legs and some shrimp." Leaning back to cross her legs. "You know that's all I know how to cook."

True….. She do have a point.

"Sounds good to me." Tilting her cup back as she gulped the strong substance down. Frowning through the burning sensation she felt in the back of her throat. "Smooth." Singing in a burping harmony. "Let me give him a call."

"You truly are all woman." Jasmine joked.

Reaching for her cellular phone. Shelly wondered what Bernard was up to anyway. She realized the only time they communicate with one another is when she initiates it. And for this to be a relationship, he sure has a way of making her feel she's in it alone.

"Thanks Jazz. I really appreciate this and all you do for me when it comes to my relationship."

"Don't mention it." Making her way into the kitchen. "It's the least I can do for all the mess Mario put us threw."

"You're right. You owe me."

As she scrolled threw her contacts. Shelly remembered the previous weekend she called and he was hanging with the fellas. He stated they were at the club. At least that's what he told her. Telling her earlier that day, he would be staying home in bed. Therefore, they didn't get a chance to speak long because he claimed he was sleepy. Since the team practiced their drills a couple hours over, preparing for the game that following week. He couldn't fathom sleep deprivation any longer. But, little did she know he had other arrangements. And no intentions of canceling them.

"Hello." A voice came through the receiver. Shocked because she assumed he would send her to the answering machine. Clearing her throat. She proceeded with her inquiry.

"Are you busy?" Embarrassed by the burp that followed.

"Naa, not really."

"Excuse me."

"What's up?"

"Well, Jazz and I planned on cooking dinner tonight and I was wondering if you weren't doing anything. Would you like to come over?" Hesitant because she knows it's never left and right with him.

"Sounds bout right." Rubbing his stomach. "I'd be over there in a few. Text me the address."

"Okay, see you in a bit."

Excited, Shelly sprung out of her seat and started cleaning. Wanting to make sure everything was decent and in order for when he arrived. She felt the need to make a good impression on him with the way her friend house appeared. Being this would be his first time there, she wanted him to feel as comfortable as possible.

"He said he'd be here in a few."

"Ok, let me get this pot started."

The music was flowing, Shelly was vacuuming, and Jasmine was tossing every seasoning she laid her eyes on in the pot. When a knock came at the door. Eager, Shelly let go of the machine and ran to answer it. Fluffing her hair and smearing the sweat from her forehead using her hands to do so. She took a deep breath and reached for the handle.

"Hey!" She greeted as the door flung open. "Come in." Revealing all thirty-twos.

"What's up."

"I can't get a hug? And I'm the one that's feeding you!" Fed up with the way he'd been treating her. "That's rude." Shifting her body to the left. "I shouldn't have to ask for affection. It should come automatically. Who does that?"

As he leaned in to hug her Jasmine walked through the kitchen to check on the pot, when she noticed Bernard standing in her living room.

"Oh, hey Nard!" With a big grin on her face.

"What's up shawty." Greeting her as he walked to the table. "What y'all cook and decided to invite a nigga over to chill and shit." Feeling some kind of way.

"We were bored and I wanted to see you. Since we didn't want to spend any money, Jazz suggested I invite you over instead. With us really not having time for one another lately. I figured her suggestion was a great idea." Emphasizing great.

"Oh."

Bernard didn't stick around to long after dinner, because he had a emergency phone call to attend to. So he say. Jasmine asked Shelly if she could ride with her to pick up Mario. She had to drop him off for work and didn't want to take that drive by herself. You never know what stunts he'd pull when they're alone. And with the history he had of acting out, she knew he wouldn't be over the top with Shelly around.

"Dinner was delicious. I really appreciate it, cause I didn't know what I was going to eat today."

As Shelly walked Bernard to the door. She hugged him before he stepped away and planted a kiss on his cheek. You could sense the distance between the two.

"You saw that?" Shelly asked as she put the latch on the door.

"Yeah. Y'all pathetic." *You can tell he cheating on her, and she just as gullible as they come.* "Why y'all act like y'all ain't got nothing to say to each other?" She asked. Wondering how they relationship is lasting without communication. Mario may have been crazy and they have there ups and downs. But, she could at least say when they are on good terms they can laugh with one another. "I started feeling uncomfortable. I was like 'dag'. They dating and they don't even have conversation. Do y'all have anything in common?"

"Not really." Concerned that her relationship may be based on lust and not love. "Now you see what I've been talking about."

"If I didn't know you guys were together. I would've thought y'all were just friends or something."

"I don't know. I told you he hardly talks to me and he always on that phone." Blind to the obvious signs in front of her face.

"Girl, I didn't think it was that bad. I thought you were over exaggerating. You know how you be over reacting, until I saw it with my own eyes. You need to figure out what you going to do before it's to late."

"What you mean."

"You need to decide if this relationship something you want and if it is, you need to do something to get his attention back on you. I don't want to put the wrong idea in your mind so I wont suggest my assumption. But, you need to get out of la la land and handle your business."

"I just needed somebody else to see what was going on and tell me I wasn't being insecure."

"Don't think negative. You just not giving him any notions for him to focus his attention on you. Once you get that in line, you guys should be fine. Come on, before Mario start blowing up my phone."

"Right…"

Pulling in the driveway, they saw Mario standing by the mailbox talking on his cell phone. As he made his way to the driver's seat, Shelly and Jasmine rotated seats. Shelly got in the back and Jasmine moved to the passenger. After he shuts his door the quarrel had begun.

"What took you so long?" Slapping the stirring wheel. Placing the vehicle in reverse. Looking back as he backed into the street.

"We were cleaning up before my aunt got home." Submissively answering. "You know she was coming back in town at 4:00p.m. If we left that house in a mess, I couldn't keep the truck."

"I was supposed to be there at 3:00p.m. Jasmine! It's 2:57p.m!" He howled as he merged onto the expressway.

Shelly was looking out the back window, focusing her attention on what took place earlier that day with Bernard. She couldn't figure why he treated her the way he do. When she gives him her last and try to make herself so easy to love. Tuning them out. She prayed and asked God to show her the things she needed to see. In the mist of her prayer, she felt a slight jerk. With her attention back on what was taking place in her current reality. Shelly realized Mario and Jasmine were arguing and he wasn't paying any mind to the road. He continued to drive recklessly as if he didn't have a care if another car hit them or the opposite. Frightened and completely helpless in this situation. Shelly begged God to let this crazy man get them to their destination safely.

At last off the interstate. Mario turns into the nearest shopping center that sat adjacent to his job.

"Give me yo debit card!"

"No!" Jasmine refused.

"Well fuck you then bitch!" He screamed. Slamming the door as he walked away. Shook up, Shelly climbed out of the car and sat in the driver's seat. Closing the door. She was as stiff as stiff could get. Nervous, scared, and confused. Shelly made an attempt to drive but for some reason her arms wouldn't respond. Looking over at Jasmine who was crying hysterically. Shelly noticed her hands were shaking as well.

"I thought this was the end Shell." Moving her lips only.

"I did to." She agreed. "When I tell you I saw my life flash before my eyes when we were on that highway. I just knew he was finna take us out." Shaking her head in disbelief. "What were you guys arguing about?" Resting her upper body on the stirring wheel.

"He was mad because we were late picking him up and I wouldn't give him no money." She explained as she wiped the tears that continued to fall. "That's my hard earned money! And if I don't want to give it to him! I don't have to! He got life fucked up!" Cursing as if he was on the receiving end of her frustration. "And to top it off, he got the nerve to try and kill us!" Getting angrier by the second. "Again!" She repeated. "Again Shelly!" Looking to her friend for understanding.

"I told you to leave him alone." Judging her decision to continue to date this guy. "But you never listen to me. You never listen!" She screeched. "Now look!" Bucking on Jasmine because she felt confrontational from the experience she'd encountered. "We stuck here scared! Can't even drive back to the house cause his stupid ass want to act a fucking fool over some got damn money! Really! Where they do that at?"

"That's petty!" Jasmine added. Roused from the discussion of the situation they were facing.

Shelly made another attempt to get back to Jasmines house. But, this time she prayed to calm her nerves.

NOT ANYMORE

"Ohhh, Arnez!" Jasmine whispered as she rolled continuously in bed. "I'm sooo happy we decided to make this thing official baby." Giggling as she found herself trapped in between the sheets. "I love you so much big daddy!" Admiring him while he dressed for work. He may have not been the tallest or the skinniest guy Jasmine had ever dated. But, with his baby smooth chocolate skin and his Casanova demeanor. Arnez could charm the panties off any damsel.

"I love you to sugar bear." He joked. Chuckling as he imagined how she would look in her senior years. "I have a few errands I need to run. Therefore, I'd see you at the club later. Right?"

"You know I'll be there." Serenading her rsvp. "I'm missing my papa already." She assures him. Puckering her lips for him to kiss before he walked out the door. "Ooo, I stank!" Getting a big whiff of her body as the covers slide off. "That's one thing about men. They never tell you when you're smelling a little funk-ta-fide!" She giggled. "Men."

While running her bath water. Jasmine over heard the doorbell ring. Unsure of whom it could've been, because she wasn't expecting any company. And, Arnez had his own key. She couldn't think for the life of her who it could

103

possibly be. "It better not be one of them helfas popping up over here without calling me first. They know I don't play that shit." She murmured. "I shouldn't even answer." Contemplating whether or not she wanted to answer it. As Jasmine made her way through the living room. She stopped to turn the radio down, because she had it blasting as if she was in the night club.

"Who is it?" Pulling the curtain back so she could get a good look at the invader.

Because whom ever it was chose to stand on the right end of the porch and her window sits on the left. She couldn't see who it was interrupting her alone time. Since there wasn't a peep hole in the door. She had no other choice but to go ahead and prop it open. "How may I help you?" She asked as the door swung open receiving the shock of her life.

"Damn baby girl!" Admiring her assets which were bursting out of her bath robe. Hips and all. "Somebody must've told you I was on my way." Slapping his hands together as he slammed his right foot forcefully into the concrete.

"What the fuck!" She shouted sarcastically. Stunned because the only thing that played on her brain was 'how did he find me'. "How'd you get my address?" Demanding an answer from her uninvited guest. Shifting her weight to the right side of her body, while placing her left hand on her waist.

"Is this how you greet your man when he comes home?" He replied flirtatiously. Smiling like he stole Christmas. Shaking his head as he stared Jasmine in the eyes.

"My man!" Still giving him attitude. "NIGGA PLEASE!" Yelling as she attempted to slam the door in his face. "Hell you talking bout!" Tuhh….. "My man." The nerve of him. "My man just left! Something you about to do right now! So go ahead and follow the mother fucking leader my nig." He must be out his crackle lacking mind if he thinks he can just pop up over here unannounced and start calling me baby and junk! And to top it off. How the heck did this loon find me? She thought. He look like he's been lurking around the neighborhood.

"Not so fast baby girl." He warned abruptly. Shoving his foot in the door.

Fearing what he may do to her and not understanding where his thoughts lye. Jasmine's safety precaution led her to start walking backwards down the hall. But, Mario came in and closed the door.

"Don't act as if you don't miss me." Turning the latch to lock the door. "I can tell how much that body misses this dick though." He continued. Turning in her direction.

"And how you figure that?" Playing along with his shenanigans. Buying herself some time until she could grab something to wop him with.

"The shortness of that robe you're wearing tells me everything I need to know. Whoever hitting it, ain't beating it hard enough. Cause ain't no way you'd be answering my door with a robe revealing that much of that ass in my house." Laying down the law like the man she knew him to be. "Plus, not knowing who you're opening it for." Sizing her up. "Ha!" He laughed. "Can't be dicking ya right."

Unimpressed by the way she allowed another man to take his place. Mario would've had more respect for the guy if he was actually running his household like a man was supposed to. In his opinion. Instead, he's letting the pussy make the rules for him. That's a sign of weakness.

"How did you find me?" Eyes locked on one another.

"I mean, you made it pretty easy if you ask me." Sliding his keys in his back pocket. "One night, I'm down at 'The Spot' chilling. I look over and who I see. Just as I thought to come speak. I saw o'l dude walk up on you."

105

He explained. "At first I was like it's cool. But then I thought about it for a second and I was like hell nawl! That's my pussy! I own that!" Taking charge of the conversation. "From then on I watched you. Once I got the feel of your schedule. It led me to where we're standing now." Telling her nonchalantly. Continuing to follow her down the dark path.

"So you've been stalking me?" Blushing at the thought of a man actually having such interest in her that he results to stalking.

"Ha! Haaa…. I wouldn't call it stalking."

"Well, what do you justify it being?" Leaning against the wall now that the path had come to an end.

Finally Mario pressed himself against her and caressed her leg.

"You want to know what I call it?" He asked as he continued to fill her up.

"What's that?" Boldly questioning his intent.

"I call it taking back what's rightfully mine." Lifting her body as he aggressively kissed her. "Now stop running from this dick girl."

Attempting to push him away. Jasmine effortlessly gave in. Because he was so strong, a part of her was turned on by his actions. Even though, she hated he had been stalking her. She just couldn't fight the urge to fuck his brains out for doing so. To her, he deserved every bit of his reward for hunting this cat down. Unlike Arnez, Mario knew exactly how Jazz liked to be pleased. He knew she liked it ruff and when he dumps it deep. The thought of his dick being forced on her, made her box even wetter. After hours of passionate sex. Jasmine immediately fell asleep with Mario still inside of her. Unaware of the time when she awoke. The sex-capade started once more.

The door shuts but no one could hear the sound. Arnez placed his keys on the end table by the door as he made his way through the house. He searched room from room wondering what happened to her. Starting to get a little worried, puzzled on why she didn't show up like they agreed. He figured maybe she fell asleep. Even if she wasn't going to come, it wasn't like her to not call and let him know. Dialing her cell once again to see if she would answer. Arnez heard the muzzled sound of it's ringing, coming from the kitchen. By him being able to see directly into the kitchen from whist he stood. There was no need to go in there, because she wasn't there.

"Jasmine!" He called out for her.

Tapping on the bathroom door as he walked towards the further rooms in the house. When he didn't receive a response, he figured maybe she did decide to turn in early. Tired from a hectic night, he planned on letting it go and getting himself some rest as well. Turning on the hall light, Arnez noticed her bathrobe was laying in the middle of the floor.

"This girl right here. I tell ya." Bending down to pick up the robe as he peered into the room.

Looking down he notices a male shoe lying at the door. But was certain it wasn't his because he doesn't own a pair of dirty sneaks. As he flipped the switch on his bedroom wall, his eyes began to water as his heart sank to the pit of his stomach. He couldn't believe what he saw before him. Never in a million years would it ever cross his mind that something like this could happen to him. But as they say 'never say never'.

"What the fuck!" He yelled. With a look of disgust and disbelief written on his face. Scaring Mario and Jasmine out of their sleep.

As both wrestled to cover their naked bodies. Jasmine attempted to explain. She didn't know how to lead with her apology, but she tried anyway.

"Baby, it's not what you think." Crying frantically. Trying to reason with an unexplainable scene. "Please let me explain." She begged. Clutching the spread in her hands as she struggled to gain control over her wobbly legs while she stood.

"Why they always asking to explain some shit!" Reacting like a mad man. "Ain't shit you can do to explain to me what I'm seeing right now!" He shouted. "Explain what! Bitch you ain't got shit to say to me!" Fussing as the flood ran freely down his cheeks. "You got to be out your rabbit ass mind, to think I'm going to sit here and let you explain anything to me and think I'ma believe the shit! When it's as transparent as water, what's going on. I've seen all I needed to see." Throwing his hands up in the air. "And ain't shit you can say to justify why you in bed with this nigga! In my house at that! In my mother fucking bed!" Provoked by her attempt to make him appear incompetent. "You can gon' somewhere with all that bullshit right there JAZZ! Straight up!" Slamming the door in the wall.

"But I'm sorry!" Pleading with him as she shed her crocodile tears. "It was a mistake. You got to believe me Arnez. I'd never do anything intentional to hurt you. I swear I wouldn't baby."

"A mistake!" Mario butted in.

If looks could kill. The way he cut her with his eyes would've took her life at that moment. She boldly stood in both their faces and lied. He knew it wasn't a mistake. And for her to cry wolf because the Sheppard returned home and caught her in her dirt. She was using those words as her plan for redemption. If he had anything to do with it, in which he does. This bitch was not getting away Scott-free. She was caught red handed and she was not about to deny his dick.

"Bitch please!" Dismissing her with the motion of his hand. "Miss me with all that fuckery right there! Save that for somebody who gives a shit!" Turning his back towards them. "Pack ya shit and get the hell up out my house!" Pointing towards the door. "And to think I told you I loved you just this morning! Bitch! Swear!" Slamming his fist in the wall.

"A mistake!" Mario boasted as he zipped his pants. "It didn't seem like a mistake to me when yo ho ass was riding this dick!" Shaking his legs to adjust the fit of his jeans. "She wanted this dick just as much as I wanted that puss." Putting emphasis on 'puss', because he knew that thang was biting. "I couldn't tell she didn't by how wide she spread them legs and how deep she begged ya boy to take it." Brushing his chest off as if dust was on him to make a statement that he do what he do and he does it well. "Obviously, you ain't hitting something right." He continued. "From the way that puss leaked for me brah." Speaking to Arnez like they were homeboys. "Ha, haa. Felt like that shit ain't been touched since the last time I hit." Before Mario could speak another word. Arnez jumped him.

"Stop it!" Jasmine screamed.

Blow after blow Arnez and Mario were throwing hits repetitiously at one another. After the first blood shed, Jasmine dialed for the authorities. When Mario got free, he ran out the back door.

"Where he go?" Wiping the blood from the side of his face.

"He's gone baby." Using her hand to wipe the speckle off his lip in efforts to assist.

"Get out!" Pushing her hands away from him.

"I'm sorry baby! Please don't be like this! We can work through this!" Reaching out to him.

"Get the fuck out my house!" Pointing his finger aggressively towards the door.

At that moment Jasmine started packing her things. Before she reached the door, she turned towards him with eyes of pity.

"I love you Arnez."

"Love don't live here anymore." He told her as he eased himself down on the couch.

"I can't believe this." She cried. "How did I allow this to happen?" Questioning herself over and over as she replayed the image of Mario in her mind when she first answered the door for him. "What was I thinking?" Rocking back and forth in the seat of her beamer. Wishing she had a second chance to relive those moments and play the hand she was dealt differently. "How could I let this mess happen?"

Jasmine reached in her purse in search of her cellular phone to call the only person she knew that could make things better.

"Yeah."

"Shelly."

"Yeah."

"Where are you? I'm on my way."

"What's wrong?" Hearing the pain in her best friends voice.

"I really need to come over right now." She sniffled. Trying to control the snot that was pouring out her nostrils. "Shelly, I have no where else to go!" She cried. "I messed everything up so bad Shell!" Barely able to understand the words coming out of her own mouth.

"Why you sound like you out of breath? And stop yelling in my ear woman!"

"I really messed up this time Shell. I don't know how to fix it."

"What are you talking about now?" Uninterested in the dramatics because it's always drama with Jasmine. It seemed as if she was a magnet to bullshit. Wherever she walked, bullshit wasn't too far behind.

"It's so much going on right now. I don't even know where to begin."

"Well you need to tell me something, if you trying to come over here."

"It's not that simple."

"It can't be that bad, I know."

"Arnez caught me and Man having sex at the house." After hearing a thump come through the phone. She realized Shelly dropped it on the floor. "Hello." Listening to her friend fumble the phone in her hands.

"I'm back."

"And he put me out, Shell!"

"What!" In disbelief. "He did what!" Still trying to process the information she received. "You got caught doing what! Mario? What!"

"Yes, and I really need my friend right now without all the judging."

"How the heck y'all get caught having sex?" Feeling the room spin. Stressing over the details of this pathetic situation. "And how the heck he end up at your house?" Wanting to crush her phone with her bare hands so she couldn't receive anymore calls that would cause her blood pressure to rise.

"I will explain everything when I get there. Where are you?"

"I didn't know y'all were talking again."

"I will tell you everything. Just tell me where you're at!" Gripping the clutch to shift gears.

"I'm at mama house right now. They released Nette today." She continued. "Just go to the house and I'll be there in the morning. The spare is in the plant."

"Okay, and thank you."

"Yeah."

Hanging up the phone, Shelly stared at her sister. Still trying to process every thought she had flowing in her mind. One thought at a time. She never suspected Jasmine cheating, and then with Mario of all people. No one could've prepared her for that low blow. Then again, Jasmine never told her about dating Arnez when they first linked up. She realized this was the second time Jasmine had kept her out of the loop. Wondering what else has she been hiding from her.

"Damn." She said. Staring off into space while pushing the 'end'

111

button. "Jazz just got caught with Mario." Laying the phone beside her.

"Mario!" Candice shouts in disgust. "I wonder how that came about."

"I'm not sure. But however it happened, Arnez put her out."

"Say what….. She was at his house?"

"That's what she told me"

"That's fucked up."

"I know." Shaking her head. "Jasmine can do some jacked up stuff but I would've never thought she would do something like this." Sucking her teeth. "And definitely not to Arnez after all they went through to try an keep their relationship private in the beginning. I thought this was it for her." Shrugging her shoulders. "But I guess not."

"I mean, if you gon' do some sneak shit like that. At least, you could've had the audacity to do it somewhere else." Candice added. "Then of all places, his crib! If that ain't grimy, I don't know what to call it." Crossing her legs as she straightened the pillow behind her back. "And then for her to do it to Arnez. Of all people she could've crossed." Instigating the seriousness of the crime Jasmine committed. "She chose him." *Damn…* "What she gon' do?" Looking to her sister to put her curiosity to rest.

"I don't know. But, I told her she could stay at my house for a while."

"What you plan on doing about Nette?"

"What you mean?" Wondering how her name came up. "What about Nette?"

"Are you going to tell her the truth?"

"The truth about what?"

"About you being her mom and all."

"No! And you better not either!" Angry because Candice kept pressing the paternity issue. "Didn't mama tell you to drop the subject?"

"Yeah."

"Therefore, drop it then!"

Pulling in the breezeway, Shelly could sense this was going to be a long day. Jasmine still had her luggage in her vehicle and she was partially parked in the grass. Walking in the house. Shelly spotted her friend gazing out the living room window, listening to love songs, propped in her recliner. She didn't walk in right away. Instead, she stared at her for a second to try and muscle up some genuine sympathy. Which was hard to do because she felt Arnez was a good guy and Jasmine took advantage of the situation he created for her. Wondering how could she risk being happy for someone who made her life a living hell.

"You know that music don't do nothing but make things worse." Shelly informed her, but Jasmine said nothing. "So what happened?" Not one utter. Just complete silence. "Are you just going to sit there or are you going to fill me in on what's going on?"

But Jasmine never turned around to acknowledge Shelly's presence in the room. She tilted her head to the right to rest it on the arm of the chair and confessed emotionlessly.

"Arnez caught me and Mario in bed together."

"See that's the part I can't seem to wrap my fingers around. How did Man even become a factor again?" She attacked directly. Dropping all chances of feeling remorse. "Since when have you been talking to him?" Completely confused on what's going on. "And of all people you could've cheated with. You chose Man! Come on now. You can do better then that."

"See, that's the thing Shell. I haven't been talking to him." She explained as more tears fell.

Not understanding what Jasmine meant. Shelly got more confused than she was in the beginning.

How can someone get caught having sex with another person, if they claim they haven't been dealing with them? I'm really beginning to think she's trying to play me like

I'm stupid.

"If y'all haven't talked. Then how you get caught with him?"

"Because, Mario been stalking me. That's how he ended up over there."

"What!"

"Yeah, he rang the doorbell and he started telling me all this stuff about him following me and this pussy his. And it went from there."

"You mean to tell me. All it took was for this man to tell you he own your body and you start spreading your legs east to west. What the hell Jasmine!"

"I know, I know. But Shell, you know how I get when I'm around Man. I can't help it."

"That don't even make sense!" Looking around for the nearest shot glass. "Listen at how you sound right now!" Voice elevated to the max. "You haven't talked to this man or been with him in God knows how long. And all of a sudden he pops up and say a few words and your panties start dropping." Grabbing the vodka off the coffee table. "That shit sounds ridiculous!" Drinking it straight from the bottle. "I can't believe you Jay!" Clearing her throat. Taking pleasure in the burning sensation that flowed down her throat. "That's foul. Especially on your behalf. Defiantly, when you're the one that's involved with someone else."

"Don't you think I know that already!"

"How you plan on explaining this to Arnez? How you expect him to even understand what happened? Cause I'm gon' keep it real with you. If I was him and you told me some shit like this, I'd think you was a ho. That's just me being real. Off top, no second guessing." Sitting on the sofa hunched over with her legs wide as to be impersonating a man.

"I tried to explain what happened. But, he won't let me." In tears again after realizing the extent of damage she had done.

Still looking over at Jasmine propped in her recliner. Shelly thought to tell her to save the tears because it was to late for that. Her relationship was over. There was nothing she could do to fix it, except let time work everything out. Instead she chose to say nothing because she wouldn't want anyone to kick her while she was down. When you think you know someone, they always continue to prove to you that you don't. Realizing no matter how long you've known them. You'd never fully know the real person on the inside or what they're capable of doing.

"I don't blame him for not listening." She admitted. "Cause if he would've heard the truth. He probably would've tried to kill you too." Taking another hit from the clear magic in the bottle. "What surprises me still, is the fact he let you walk out the house." Clapping her hands. Giving Jasmine a round of applause for escaping another possible near death experience.

"Shell, the thing that hurt me the most about everything that went down." Leaning over the arm rest. "Is when he started crying."

"Who?"

"Arnez."

"Really...."

"Yeah, why would I lie?"

"You do know what that means, right?" Punching her left hand.

"What?"

"Obviously, you're still very much in love with Mario. And if you tell Arnez what really went down. It will be crystal to him as well."

"But I'm not in love with him Shell! I love Arnez!"

"I can't tell."

"But I do! I really do!"

"If that's your story. Then I'd stick to it if I were you." Peering through the crystal. "If he finds out. He will never be able to look at you the same. That's even if he does decide to reconsider. The only thing I can advise you to do. Is give him his space and see what happens." Laying the bottle sideways on the couch. "Until then, prepare yourself as if this relationship is over boo." Stretching as she arose from her seat. "Damn, and he cried to." Shaking her head as she exited the room.

"Umm hum....."

"I don't know about this one girly." Standing in the doorway. "Bernard supposed to be coming back from Vermont tonight. I'd stay with him for a while and let you chill here until everything blows over." She offered. "But, if you need me. You know I always have my cell. So, holler if you need me."

BOILING

"Mario, Yella, and I are going to the mall. It really, really would make me happy if you would ride with us."

"I bet it would." Wanting to say no.

"Pleeessassseee Shell. Come with us." She begged. In hopes it would convince her to say yes. "I reeeeaaalllllly don't want to be by myself with them." Twisting her body. "You know he gon' start flexing since Yella with us. I need someone there with me to ignore him with."

"And out of all people you could've asked. You picked me." She giggled. Finding humor in the way Jasmine graveled at her to tag along.

"I know if you came, we could leave them and shop around on our own. We ain't even got to be bothered with him." Trying to sweeten the pot in efforts of making her want to tag along.

"That's what you're saying now." Seeing straight through her scheme.

"Please, Shell." Pulling on her arm. "I'm begging for this one favor." Tilting her head back and forth as she continued to pull on Shelly's arm.

"I'll think about it."

"I'll buy you whatever you want." Resulting to bribery. She knew begging wasn't going to do the trick and she didn't want to bring out the big guns unless it was necessary. And seeing Shelly wasn't budging. She had no other choice but to offer leverage.

Jack pot. Shelly sang in her mind.

"Okay, I'll ride." Bubbling up with excitement.

"Now that's trifling." Wanting to call Shelly a gold digger now that she'd agreed to go. Only, because a free purchase was offered. "It took me to bribe you for you to say you'd come with me."

"Duh…" *Of course. What she thank this is.* Looking at Jasmine with a blank stare. "We both know this ain't finna be no walk in the park riding with them."

"Wheew….." *I guess she do make a good point.* "I owe you big time for this."

"Show you right." Rubbing her hands together with a devilish look in her eye. "And you about to pay up, soon as we get there." Chuckling in her evil voice.

When they got in the car, Mario was playing one of their favorite songs on the radio. Shelly looked in the mirror as she sang and caught him staring her smack dab in the face. Tooting her nose up at him. She turned away. *I wonder how long his ass been looking at me.* She murmured. Glancing out the window as she thought about how trifling he was. And how much of a menace he is. When she first laid eyes on him. It was as if 'trouble' was tattooed on his forehead. Never in a million years would she have ever guessed 'trouble' would become a part of her life. Since Jasmine was her best friend. Shelly ignored and dismissed his childish antics as if it never happened. Being the good friend she considered herself to be. She never mentioned the times Mario tried to make several advances at her either. She knew it would only cause more strife then good.

Riding down Peachlee, Shelly and Yella were conversing in the back seat. Cracking a few jokes, enjoying one another company. Since it's not often they see each other. When she realized he wasn't half as bad as Man. She figured she'd welcome his company.

"What you been up to?" He asked. Looking down at her breast.

"Oh, nothing really." Noticing where his eyes were locked. "Just work and home. You know how I do." *Bastard.* Withdrawing her first assumption and deeming him to be the pervert out the two.

"Check, check. So tell me something about yourself. Things I don't already know." Making himself more comfortable by crouching down in the seat.

"I got a man." She laughed.

"That's cold. Real cold, but cute."

"I know!" Chumping him off in a coy way.

"You wild."

"But you like it though." She flirted.

"I never said that."

"You didn't have to." Shaking her head. "I can tell."

"And how is that?" Rubbing his chin as he sized her up.

"See, there you go asking to many questions."

"Ha, haaa... I see how you like to do."

"And what that supposed to mean?"

"Curious aren't we?"

"You ain't shit." She laughed.

"I'm just doing you." Sliding his hand underneath her chin. Wanting to steal a kiss. "I like them feisty."

"Well, this one taken."

"Umm hum."

"What that supposed to mean?"

"I didn't mean nothing by it Ms. Lady." Using sarcasm to explain himself. "I'm just saying. For somebody to claim their taken. She sure is flirting with me. And the way I see it, anybody can claim to be in a relationship. But, if there's no ring or contract signed. Persuasion can be a fun game to play."

Letting his words marinate, Shelly was left speechless. For the life of her she couldn't think of anything to say to defend herself. Because Jasmine and Mario started arguing, they cut their conversation short and focused their attention to the front. Both could sense the intensity of this particular argument because Jasmine was cursing more then she had in the past. Before any of them knew it. A wad of money flew out the window.

"What in the world!" Shelly yelled.

"Brah!!!! For real yo!!!" Angry with Mario for tossing the money out the window. "What's your problem man?" Leaning between the seats. Heart broken because he felt if Mario was a good friend he would've given him the money. Knowing he needed it. "What's really good?" Watching several big faces float away in the wind.

"Man, fuck this bitch!"

Did he really just throw some money out the window? Shelly asked. Referencing the question to herself.

"I know my eyes got to be playing tricks on me!" Using her shirt to wipe her glasses. "I think my glasses greased up or something. Maybe I need a new pair, cause I know this nigga didn't just do what I think he did!" Smearing the lens with all her might, trying not to leave not one trace of dust on them.

Pressing down on the accelerator. Mario sped up. He didn't care if the police pulled him over or not. He was bucking the system and nobody could stop him. People were moving their vehicles to the side to let him pass, because he was tailing everyone in front of him.

"She always find something to complain about! Saying she need money for this and need money for that!" He ranted. "When a nigga try and make something shake. She act like the shit ain't good enough! Like it's never enough!" Pointing his finger in Jasmine's face. "Bitch you don't know what the fuck I have to go through to come up with this money to give your ungrateful ass!" Pushing his finger in her face while they awaited the light to turn green. "You don't know what a nigga out here risking! And have the nerve to complain!"

"Ion give a fuck!" She barked back at him. Wanting to grip the stirring wheel and make him crash. "That's your choice!" Forcing his hand out her face. "Not mine!" Pointing back at him. "I ask! I don't care how you get it. You just need to make sure I get it!" Turning around in her seat facing the window.

"And have the nerve to say it's not enough. Like I tried your motherfucking ass!" Feeling some type of way. "Fuck you bitch!" Frowning as if he'd just eaten a lemon head. "If it ain't enough! Go sell some pussy then ho!" He suggested. "You ain't getting shit else from me ever!" Emotional because he thought giving her the money would make her happy. Even though, he couldn't come up with the whole amount she asked for. He figured by having a portion would make her smile. But it was another failed attempt to satisfy another ungrateful woman.

"I understand you're mad bro. But, why do something you're going to regret later?"

"Since it ain't enough. I said fuck it. Won't none of us have it!"

"Dude you tripping." Shaking his head. "Over a bitch at that!" Trying to relate to what his friend could possibly be going through. "If shorty didn't want the money. Then you should've kept it yourself." *Sensitive ass.* "Not throw it out the window." *Stupid.*

With all the ruckus going on in the car. Shelly continued to watch all the money float away in the air. People were pulling over, getting out of their vehicles to catch whatever they could grab. It was raining men figuratively speaking. And everyone wanted their share.

"Ain't that about a blimp." She said. "All cause a nigga balls bigger than his dick." Resting her cheek in her hand. "Bitch ass." Watching the crowd go into a frenzy.

Soon after they arrived at Nexwell Mall. Because everyone was mad at Mario, none of them spoke a word while getting out of the car. Mario walked off and left the rest of the crew together. That meant Yella was stuck with the girls. Because he didn't have a cell phone. There was no way for him to call and see where Mario went off to. And since Mario tossed all the cash out the window. He didn't have a way to eat dinner either. Therefore, he was at the mercy of two angry women.

"I'm hungry. Let's go to the food court real quick." Jasmine suggested. "After that we can go try and find me a new phone."

"Okay." Shelly said as she followed Jasmine up the escalator. "Have you decided which company you were going to switch to?"

"Not yet." Looking down at the phone she had already. "We can just walk around and see who have the better prices. I do know I want something touch screen this time." Walking toward the food court entrance. "Are you hungry?"

"Yea, a little bit." Rubbing his stomach. Which was making loud fart noises.

"Well you can have some of my food then." Shelly offered.

"I'm sorry this happened Shell. I shouldn't have asked you to come." Guilty, because she knew this was one of the reasons Shelly didn't want to come in the first place.

Mario didn't posses a civilized bone in his body. Not even when they were alone. Shelly was Jasmines best friend, but she didn't like the fact that she had to choose between the two. Either be with the man she loved or spend time with her friend. On the days she wanted to be with them both. She knew the idea was kind of far fetched, because Shelly wanted nothing to do with him. And by her coming with them to the mall. It made Jasmine happy because she thought for once she could have them in the same area. But disaster seemed to have tagged along as well.

"It's ok." Comforting her. "I sensed something like this was bound to happen anyway. I knew that monkey couldn't stay hidden for long. But it came sooner than I expected."

"I still want to apologize. Because you wouldn't be in this mess if I never invited you."

"True, but it's cool. Long as you hold up your end of the bargain then everything is a.o.k."

Looking around at all the options they had to choose from. Jasmine couldn't decide which was better. She loved food. And anything that was already hot, she wouldn't complain. Whether it was Asian, Chinese, Mexican, Jamaican, Cashion, or American. Food was her life.

"What you got a taste for?"

"Ion know ma." Looking around to see what appealed to him the most. "Since you buying, I'll eat whatever you decide to get. Beggars can't be choosers. You feel me."

"I know. But, I at least wanted to have an idea of some of the things you liked." She explained. Undecided on what she wanted as well. "Jazz!"

"What's up?"

"What you eating?"

"You already know. Taco Spell girl!!!!!!" Dancing in the middle of the floor.

"Taco Spell!" Frowning at the thought of eating those greasy tacos.

"You need to switch it up."

"I need my sour cream and guacamole after all this drama." Laughing as she walked over to Taco Spell. "The only thing I need to be concerned about is having to use the bathroom after. Anything other then that is irrelevant."

"I think I got a taste for Chinese." Shelly contemplated. "Is that cool with you?"

"I'll eat whatever."

"Bet. Do you like Crab Rangoon?"

"I never tried it."

"Cool, I'd let you taste one of mine. Instead of buying you your own."

When the three of them sat down to eat. They discussed a few other stores they wanted to visit for window shopping purposes. Yella suggested a male shoe department he wanted to look in and Shelly wanted to go see the latest bra that was released two days prior by her favorite lingerie dealer. After about five minutes into the conversation, Mario decided to come back to the group. Seeing the plate Yella was eating from angered him. He felt by this being his friend. He should've left with him, when he left the group earlier. And feeling his friend betrayed him. Out of spite, he flipped the plate on the floor.

"Brah!" Raising up from his seat. "What the fuck!" Agonized by all the rice spilled on the floor.

"Nigga fuck you!" Kicking the plate as he walked off.

"I'm getting sick of his shit!" Slamming her taco in the lump of guacamole. "I'm ready to go." Stuffing the contents in her mouth. "Come on y'all. We finna go."

"I think it's real jacked up the way he's been acting like a jerk." Making it obvious who's side he's on. "He's been doing this mess since we left my crib." Using the key to unlock the drivers door. "He tripped out for real."

"I'm sorry y'all had to go through that." Sounding like a broken record. "Mario be on some other stuff sometimes." Still making excuses for his behavior. "One minute everything's cool, then the next...." Disappointed she didn't get a chance to purchase her cellular phone.

When they got to the house, Jasmine received a text from Mario. **Mario: What took y'all so long to get here? I got here twenty minutes ago lol.**

"Bastard!"

"What?" Shelly glanced back at her from the passenger seat.

"That bastard just text me."

"What he say?" Asking sarcastically. Unbuckling her seat belt.

"He said he already at the house."

"Say what!" Slamming the door. "How he get there?"

"He said he caught a cab."

"Wow, if that ain't shady I don't know what to call it." Yella added. Shelly didn't say a word. She just shook her head and walked in the house. Because Yella stayed a few blocks over from Jasmine's house. He walked home from there.

Later on that evening, Shelly and Jasmine where at the house watching television when they heard a knock at the door. Boom! Boom! Boom! Jasmine wasn't expecting company. Therefore, she didn't know who it could've been knocking at her door so late and so random. Knowing her aunt was out of town at the time. She immediately eliminated that possibility. And it couldn't have been Shelly, because she was sitting right next to her.

"Who is that?" Shelly whispered. Clinching the bowl of popcorn.

"I don't know." Feeling as if she was reenacting a scene from the film they were watching. "Ima look out the peep hole and see."

"Deal." Agreeing with Jasmine because she was afraid to check herself. Even though, she was the closest to the door. "They would come a knocking when we watching a scary movie with all the freaking lights out."

"Shh…" Shushing Shelly. "I don't want them to hear us talking."

"But the T.V. on."

"So, everybody leaves their T.V. on." Hunching down low to the floor. "Just shut up."

As Jasmine inched towards the door. She easily tip toed till she felt the door handle on her forehead. Holding her breath the whole time as if the guest could hear her breathing. Easing up the wall until her eye met the peep hole. She turned to Shelly in a state of panic.

"Is it the police?" She whispered. Stuffing a piece of popcorn in her mouth. For she felt she was still watching the flick that was now on commercial.

"Hide in my auntie room real quick." Scurrying to remove all evidence of company being in the house.

"Why?" Watching Jasmine clean like a mad lady that's about to get caught relaxing on the job by her boss.

"It's Mario!"

"And, why do I have to hide again?"

"Because he don't like you! Duhhh!" Panicking as she straightened the coasters. "Lock the door and don't make a sound."

Unsure of why she had to hide. Shelly didn't ask any more questions. She just did what she was told. After locking the door. Shelly laid on the bed and started wondering why she felt unsafe. But then she thought back on all the previous attempts Mario made on her life and she didn't hesitate or think twice about the importance of her not being noticed.

"This nigga crazy."

Jasmine, fluffing the pillows and rushing Shelly's cup to the kitchen sink. Came back into the living room and took one last look before she opened the door. She knew if Mario saw Shelly there, things would escalate from good too bad within seconds. And she'd had enough drama for the week. Removing the key chain, Mario pushed past her and started looking around. Investigating the room. He didn't see the popcorn anywhere but he could smell there was some.

"What took you so long to open the door?" Talking loud to make his presence known throughout the house.

"I was sleep."

"Yeah, right. And you expect me to believe that." Still looking around.

"How you gone tell me what I was doing?" Following his footsteps.

"Cause I know you lying." He accused. "Who sleeps in the middle of the day?"

"I do!" Lying with a straight face.

"Why you seem so anxious then? And why it smell like popcorn in here?"

"Whatever Mario!" *'Dag' I can't hide shit.* "Ain't nobody got time to play these games with you." Quickly changing the subject. *He need to get his butt on somewhere . Ain't nobody got time for his shit today.* "What do you want?"

"I can't miss my baby and want to come spend a little time with her?" Stating playfully as he grabbed at her waist. Grinding his body in a circular motion as he dipped low a bit. Putting on a private show for her.

"Not without calling first." Thrusting her body away from him.

"I was in the neighborhood so I decided to drop in to see what my honey was doing." Grabbing a handful of her ass.

"I don't see why." Wrestling to keep his hands off her. "We ain't talking like that no more." *He got some nerve coming up in here thinking we got something going on. After all that crap he put me through the other day. He done lost his everlasting mind.* "It's over between us." *Deal with it.* "You don't have nothing else to say to me." Walking back to the door.

"Come on Jazzy poo." He begged. "Don't be like that." Pulling her closer to him. Using his magical hands to caress her perky breast. Which were poking through her shirt, because she didn't have a bra on to tame them. "You know I need you." Bending down to greet one with his lips.

"You should've thought about that before you did what you did the other day." Gripping his head to pull him off her breast. Which he was now latched on to. Fiddling her nipple through her shirt with his tongue.

"You still mad about that?" Annoyed but still attempting to seduce. "I thought we were passed that by now." Moaning as he caressed her.

"Ha!" She blurted sarcastically. "Get your hands off of me!" She tussled. Trying to pull him towards the door.

While lying in bed. Shelly could hear everything that was taking place on the other side of the thin wall. Mario was nothing but a horn ball in her book. And for that reason she felt that's why he put up with Jasmine's temper tantrums. Suddenly the door handle started to rattle. Shelly gripped the bed spread in fear of what was to happen once he got in. Bracing herself for the inevitable.

"Why auntie door locked?" He asked deviously. "Is she in there?"

"No... So leave her door alone!"

"If she not in there like you say. Then why her door locked?"

"Because she locked it."

"Auntie! Auntie!" He yelled. As he continued to jerk at the door. He knew she was lying but he didn't know how to prove it. Jasmine had never turned down his advances for sex no matter how angry she was with him. Therefore, he knew something strange was going on. And she couldn't use being on her menstrual as an excuse, because she had that excuse last week.

Shelly could hear Mario yelling out for Jasmine aunt. Slowly feeling around for something sharp. She wanted to make sure she had something handy just in case he did get in.

"When she start doing this?"

"Since we kept going through her stuff. She put a lock on it to keep us out. Now stop before you brake it." She instructed.

After several attempts, she finally convinced him to give up and leave the door alone. Silence fell over the house and then a loud slam.

"Shelly, open the door." A whisper came from the opposite side of the door.

Angrily she got up and unlocked it. "Why you even let him in?" Peering Jasmine in her eyes.

"Don't ask me that!" Brushing her off. "I don't say nothing to you when you be going back and forth with Bernard. Do I?" Implementing reverse psychology.

"But what that got to do with anything?" Appalled, because she failed to find the relevancy of mentioning her situation. "The difference between me and you is, Nard don't try to kill me and my friends. That's your crazy man that be with that fuckery. So you can never compare me to you." Rolling her neck.

"Whatever." Staring blankly at her friend. Emotionally unattached. "I'm going to bed."

I know she didn't just walk off on me.

"Just trifling."

SPEECHLESS

The room smelt like a pound of disinfecting spray and you could hear the sound of latex gloves being slapped repeatedly on someone's arm. Reaching to grab the sanitized napkin to clean the skin of his patient. The room grew completely silent when he ripped the package open to free the pad. As the doctor pierced her skin with a butterfly needle. Sweat rolled off the patients face from all the nervousness she felt. At that moment, to her it felt like someone turned up the heat to about ninety degrees but she was baking as if it was four hundred. This woman was so shook up when the doctor left the room. Her teeth had begun chattering.

"Waiting on some shit like this. Would cause a mother fucker to have a heart attack." She said a loud. *I should've stayed home.* She thought to herself as she fumbled through the drawers of the cabinet. In search of some gloves she could take home. "I wonder which one those band aids are in. I know I need some of those." Sliding each one open with caution as much as possible. Trying to be as quite as she possibly could. In efforts not to attract any attention to her room.

Scrolling threw her phone to put her mind at ease. She checked her news feed on her social network to keep herself occupied, while she waited. Loosing track of time. When she saw the door swing open, it caught her off guard because it felt as if he just left. With a chart in his hands and a look that was worth a thousand words. She knew nothing good was about to come from this vist. Therefore, she knew what time it was.

It was clear something was wrong, but she kept her composure trying to give herself the benefit of the doubt. He handed her a pamphlet before he took a seat on his stool. Her world stopped as she glanced over the cover. When she focused in on the title, while the doctor spoke to her. Her brain shut down like a generator having technical difficulties.

"I'm sorry to have to break this news to you ma'am." Pausing to console her. As he grabbed her by the hand. Peering in her eyes to show genuine compassion for what he was about to say.

"But your results came back positive….." Leaning forward to give her reassurance that everything will be ok. "We can start your treatments as soon as you sign our consent form for us to treat you here in our facilities." Rubbing her hand in confidence. "The sooner we start the better chances we have of keeping your organs fully functional." Treading lightly to be sensitive to her feelings. "Many people still lead good and healthy lives after this, so don't stress yourself about it." Hoping to make her feel better in her state of loneliness. "It's treatable."

She sat there lifeless. Unable to process the image she saw and the confusion she felt. Within seconds her life changed and it only took minutes to change a lifetime. Where, when, and how it happened wasn't her concern. How she would move forward from this was the stressor.

"We will start your treatment today and you can pick up your medication from the pharmacy before you leave." Because he had the prescription written out already. He handed it to her and assisted with walking her to the checkout counter. "The nurse will schedule you an appointment to return in six weeks. We set it close because we would like to see if your body will be receptive to the dose we gave or will it reject it."

Informing her as she starred blankly into space. "Every individual is different. Therefore, we have to monitor each person as such." Nodding his head looking to get a response from her. But still nothing. "Everything will be just fine. I promise you. And a year from now, we will look back on this day and laugh." He assured her as tears formed in her eyes.

BEST FRIENDS

"I'm outside."

"Ok, here I come." *Let me check and make sure my curls still intact.* Rushing to the mirror to give herself one last and final glance, before she stepped out the house. *I scream gorgeous.* Talking to herself. Admiring every inch of her body she viewed in the mirror. *I need to get out of here, but somebody needs to pay me for looking this dag blame good. Ain't nobody dope as me, I'm just so fresh so clean.* She sang as she turned out the light.

"Damn girl!" Eyeballing her body like a snack he was ready to pop. "You look good ma." Thrilled, because he felt she was a prize he had won after playing a game at the county fair.

"Thank you."

"Smelling good to." He added.

"I try."

"So what you getting into today?" Looking Shelly up and down. Fantasizing about snatching every article she had on off. "Why you all dressed up?" Licking his lips as he continued to drool.

"Oh nothing. Just felt like getting dolled up today. I wanted to feel sexy, I guess." Rubbing her hands down the sides of her body. Tracing her frame. She could hear his phone buzzing in his jeans pocket and wondered who it could've been calling him this early in the day. As he reached down to answer it. She admired his physique as his muscles flexed.

"Hello." Turning away from her as he spoke. "Yeah, she down here." Glancing back at Shelly as he confirmed her being in his presence. "Alright." Ending the call. Walking back in her direction.

"Who was that?" Curious of who it could've been calling his phone inquiring about her.

"That was Mario."

What he want. She thought.

"He said he was on his way down here." Sliding the phone back in his back pocket.

Unsure of why Mario was asking if she was with him and his concerns about it anyway. Shelly thought to strike up another conversation but, before she could spark one Mario came rushing through the bushes. The way he launched out. She wasn't sure if she should be calm or frightened. Either way, nothing good would come from this encounter and deep down she knew something was bound to pop off. And of all days, he chose that one to come ruin.

"What the fuck you doing down here chilling with this ho?"

"Ho!" Shelly argued. "Who you calling a ho!" Knowing he was directing his accusations at her.

Yella places his arm in front of her to ease his way between the two. One thing he didn't want, was for Shelly to get hurt. Definitely not while he was around and he's responsible for her being there. And especially not over no none sense.

"Y'all fucking around now?"

"What does it matter?" Stepping up in her defense.

"You my best friend and if I don't want you hanging with this bitch then you don't fuck with her!" Claiming rights to his partner. "Like I said." Standing face to face with the man he had been friends with since the age of nine.

"You can't tell me who I can and can't fuck with!" Backing back putting space between him and Man.

"Why I can't?" Stepping closer with a intimidation attempt.

"What you so mad about it for anyway?" Questioning his motives. "Don't you got a gir-."

Before Yella could finish his statement. Mario took the beer he was holding in his hands and poured it in Shelly's hair. A long silence fell upon them and suddenly Yella reacted within a blink of an eye. He punched Mario in the face and the brawl begun.

"I can't believe he did this!" Shelly cried out.

She couldn't believe Mario came down there starting stuff, all because Yella was entertaining her company. Why was he so jealous. Walking away from the fight Shelly attempted to call Jazz. But on her first attempt, there was no answer. Dialing once again, rage sank in. As she walked home. Shelly glanced back at the boys and saw they were still at it. Some of their neighbors came out of their homes to try and break the fight up. But none were successful. You could hear the voices pleading with them to let go of one another. But Shelly never went back.

"Hello." A voice came threw her receiver.

"Girl...... Why I was down here minding my own business talking to Yella and Mario came over here starting shit. Talking about why you hanging with this ho. And then had the nerve to pour his beer on me!"

"What!" Shocked by the news. Feeling resentment towards Shelly because Mario had always wanted to be with her. But since Shelly wouldn't go for what he was offering, he tried to mess up every relationship she had.

"Yeeesssss, bitch!" Shelly explained. "Why he always somewhere hatting on some damn body?" Fed up with his childish acts to gain attention. "Like he jealous or something?" Completely unaware of why he did what he did when it came to her. For Jasmine never told her he use to complain about wishing he'd chose her.

"Stop lying." She chuckled. Not believing a word Shelly said.

Why would my man be mad because you talking to another nigga. She thought. *This bitch delusional.* Holding strong to her front.

"Why would I make something like this up?" Aggravated with Jasmines nonchalant demeanor.

"Bitch he don't want you!" In a state of denial. Wishing with every bone in her body Shelly was playing a joke on her. For it killed her over and over repeatedly at the thought of her boyfriend at another mans house fighting over a woman that wasn't her.

"What!" Not understanding how Jasmine could be angry. "Hold up, what you just say?" Looking down at her phone. "Ain't nothing like that came out my mouth first off why you over there trying to flex on somebody. I called you to put your simple ass up on game and let you know what's going on round here!"

"Don't call my phone making up stories and shit. Talking about Mario down there checking another nigga over you." Still thinking Shelly playing a joke on her, but in the back of her mind she knows she's telling the truth. "Bitch you ain't shit!"

Bitches these days....... Brushing the accusations off.

"You need to get your nose out your ass, cause you damn sho ain't all that." (Click) Jasmine hangs up.

"I know this bitch........."

Appalled, Shelly continued her journey home. "I know this bitch ain't just hang up in my face." Contemplating to herself as she tried to piece the puzzle together on what just took place. Furious not only because her supposed best friend hung up on her. But, to top it off. Her hair was ruined because of Mario.

"Am I missing something here? Did I miss the memo that this was fuck Shelly's day up or something?" In deep dialog with herself. "I think I need to reenact what just went down, or what I think happened. Because I'm beginning to feel I got this whole situation misconstrued." Pacing back and forth. "Ok. I picked up my phone first." Picking up her phone. "Then, I scrolled threw the contacts until I saw Jazz's name." Using her thumb to scroll. "I clicked 'send' to dial the number and then she answered. As I started to explain. I heard 'bitch', 'ain't shit', 'nose in ass', 'click'." With her finger in motion as she figured things out. "Let me call her back." Wanting to give her the benefit of the doubt that her phone died.

"Wooh saaaah lady, wooh saaah......" Breathing deeply to calm her nerves. *Humble yourself Shell and give her the benefit of doubt. Her call dropped, she didn't hang up on you.*

Tick! Tick! Tick! "Send." Ring! Ring! Ring! **"You have reached 671)873-2519. At the beep please leave a detailed message and press pound for delivery options when your message is complete. Beep!"**

"I'll show this bitch a BITCH." Having another conversation with herself. Prepping for the tone to leave a message. "Look here you rabbit ass bitch! I know yo scary ass sent me to the machine but that's ok ho! Cause at the end of the day. You going to need me first and Ima do the same shit you doing." She blurted. "Trust and believe me, you're going to need me. But the difference between me and you, Ima answer and still tell yo ass no." She sung. "Fuck you! Fuck yo life! Fuck yo line! Fuck yo trifling ass man! And go suck a phat sick dick bitch! Cause I'm through with yo ucky ass!"

"If you would like to leave a call back number please press star

now."

Two weeks had passed and Shelly continued to ignore Jasmine attempts to contact her. "This bitch got some nerve to try and call me now. I know she didn't think I was going to answer that easy! Especially after all this time done flown by! She should've thought about that before she sent me to that damn voice mail." Shelly babbled. "Can't wait till I see that monkey ass." Getting anxious. "She got the right one!"

The phone continued to ring and Shelly continued to ignore. After about four attempts it finally stopped.

"About time!"

Beep! Beep! (A text message came through). **Jasmine: Mario just got locked up for breaking and entering.**

"Serves his ass right. All the crap he put me through. I don't know what she telling me for. Like I'm supposed to care or something. He don't get no tears from this side of the mountain. He better go find him a river or something if he want to see some water fall."

Jasmine: Could you please call me when you get this message.

"Nope."

Shelly: Fuck you and him bitch! Loose the number.....

Jasmine: you doing all this over a nigga. Look at how petty you are. Real friends don't do stuff like that. That's why yo ass lonely now cause you always bitching over petty stuff. Grow the fuck up Shell! Bye.

Shelly: I don't know who you think you regulating on but you could've kept all that. Miss this line from yo phone boo boo.

"The nerve of this girl!" Shaking her head in disbelief.

SIGNS

As the door flung open, Shelly walked through the hall to greet Bernard as he entered. Excited to see him. All she wanted to do was feel his warm embrace. Bernard had been gone for several days, because his contract was coming to an end at the end of the season. Therefore, he had to go meet with his coach to see what their next move would be. Since Shelly had a lot of personal things going on in her life at that time, she couldn't make the trip with him. Being a loving and extremely supportive girl friend. It pained her to not have been by his side when a major decision was being made in his life. Not only will this decision they make affect Bernard, but it can possibly change her life as well.

"How was your trip babe?" Excited to lay eyes on her man.

"You can say everything went well." With a charming smile on his face.

"Well, give me all the details then?" Flopping down on the couch. "You know I'm just dying on the inside to know." Sitting in Indian style. Anxious to hear all he had to share about his trip.

"Haaa, haaaa." Swinging his duffle bag off his shoulder. "Calm down." Unable to reframe from blushing at her interest in his affairs. "I had a couple meetings the morning I arrived. The first was with coach Larry. You know he wanted to run over the plans before I spoke with anyone else. And one later on that afternoon as well. But, it was nothing your big man couldn't handle." He boasted. "I went in there and did my thing, as usual." Rubbing his chin. Boasting as he stroked his ego.

"Well....... What did you guys talk about?" She asked eagerly. Tilting her head slightly to the right as she rested it in the palm of her hand. Giving him her full attention.

"We went over some contracts that they felt would be a good opportunity for me to run with."

Damn.

"Nosey ain't you." Cutting her with his eye.

"Not really." Unsure of how she should respond to his accusation. "I need to make sure I've crossed all my t's and dotted all my I's, because this matter doesn't concern you only. It concerns both of us."

Making sure she's assertive. Therefore, he'd realize the seriousness of their situation.

"Whatever choice you make will affect not only your future but mine as well. If I'm not knowledgeable of the things that's taking place around me, or in the loop with what's going on. Then I could be s.o.l, if you make the wrong decision." Trying not to offend.

"Basically, what it all boiled down to is; either I trade or take a pay cut." Resting his elbows on his knees as he debated with his thoughts.

"Lesser pay!" Shelly yelled. "That's a chump off!" Appalled by the ultimatum they gave.

"That's what it seems like I have to do, since the contract ends at the end of this year. And they aren't trying to renegotiate with me, because of how I played these last two years. Coach offered me an opportunity to decide myself as an act of good faith."

"What a way to stick it to somebody." Shaking her head in disbelief.

"I know right." Agreeing with her while he gazed into her confused eyes.

"Are you at least excited about it?"

"Excited about what?" Unbeknownst to him of what he should be stoked about.

"About the trade!" She stated enthusiastically. "If that's what you decided." Anxious to know what his plans are.

"Yeah...... A little bit, I guess." Holding on to his words. "I haven't had time to think about it. Let alone, sit and reflect on what 'trade' actually in tells."

As Shelly and Bernard sat across from one another. There was a slight pause in time. At least that's what it felt like to them. Shelly thought of all the prospects a trade could mean for her. And couldn't help but think this could be the opportunity she had been waiting for. Wanting to leave, but never having the courage to. Out of fear of living alone. Now, that Bernard had no other choice except to pack up and go. This was her ticket out. While Shelly hovered on the good this trade would bring, Bernard felt the opposite.

"'Trade' means new city. 'New city' means new people. 'New people' means a new start. Are you ready for something like that?" Thinking she wasn't prepared to leave her family just yet.

"If I want us to work. I have to make the necessary adjustments to accommodate what we have." Hoping she's not stuffing her own foot in her mouth for that statement later. "Long as you don't lead me off a cliff." Giving him the eye.

"But, your family is here." Reminding her what she's sacrificing. "Can you deal with them not being around all the time?" Holding his breath.

Afraid because he didn't want to come off selfish because he wanted her to choose him.

"It haven't crossed my mind. But, I'm a grown woman now. With that being said, I make my own decisions. I can always call or take a trip down to see them. Definitely, when I feel like I need a get away. It would be perfect to fly back home on occasion. Only to let my hair down and leave when I'm tired of seeing them." Reassuring him that whatever decision he decided to make. She was more than prepared to make them right along with him. Shelly had every intention of being Bernard's wife in the near future. And if she wanted to keep that option open, she knew she would have to leave with him.

"You sound like you have it all figured out."

"If that's what you call it. Then, I guess I do. I think on my feet, if you haven't noticed. And besides...... I can work anywhere sense I'm my own boss. Plus, this could be my chance to expand." Viewing this mishap as a business venture.

"Yeah, I see what you mean." Imagining the possible success that could potentially come from a new client base. "My only issue I keep having with this is wondering if I'm doing the right thing."

"And what thing is that?"

"Switching to another team."

Something about leaving doesn't sit well with Bernard's gut. And people have always told him to go with his gut instinct. Having to take a pay cut was not optional. Definitely, with the load he had on his shoulders regarding Renee and the baby.

"I don't want to move. But the owners of our team has made it clear they didn't want to sign me for another season. I don't want to take the money they're offering and then regret it later. For them to offer me the amount they're offering, is a method all teams use to force players to leave.

Because they know we can't sustain our life style with it." Looking up at Shelly.

"Don't contradict yourself." She encouraged. "Always go with your first mind." Trying to lighten up the gloomy mood in the room.

"I know, but it's not all about the move." He wined.

"Well what is it?" Growing tired of hearing his excuses.

"It's about choosing another team." Sighing. "What if I don't pick the right one?" Fumbling his hands. "I can move today and play to my fullest potential and they may not think it's good enough." Looking at his hands as he jerked them back and forth. Trying to explain his thoughts to Shelly. "If that was to happen. They could bench me until next season." Weighing his options as he continued to think. "Benching me won't be good for either of us. Because that could mean I'm under the microscope for getting cut and my opportunity for another sign on will be slim to none."

"How can you predict what will happen, before any final agreements are discussed. You can't start off thinking negative, because that's hindering all the positive." Leaning over to rub his leg.

"Lets be realistic here Shell. I'm climbing the latter in age." He continued to cry. "I can't do what I did when I first started playing." Accepting father time has finally caught up with him. "I'm no spring chicken, you know."

"Don't put too much pressure in over thinking things Nard." Trying to change his outlook on things. "God knows best and he won't put nothing on you he felt you couldn't handle." Throwing in some spiritual inspiration. "So whatever the outcome, trust everything will be ok."

"I hear ya." Brushing her off. "But if this goes south. Remember, you said you wouldn't leave me."

To Bernard, everything was falling apart now that life was starting to

145

happen. Where he once was care free, things have turned for the worse. His job is unstable. The woman he was cheating with, had turned up pregnant. Age was taking a toll on his performance. And, he don't know how Shelly will react to finding out the secrets he's been keeping from her. But one things for sure, nothing good will come from any of it. Bernard Curry's days of living the fab life was coming to an end. And as the days continued to pass, his fate was no longer in his control.

"I'm going to stay here for a few days and let Jazz stay at my place until she pulls herself together. Is that okay with you?" She asked. Thinking to herself, 'he better not say no'.

"Did you really just ask me if you could stay the night?" With sarcasm. "Of course, you don't have to ask to stay here."

"You never know." Shrugging her shoulders. "You could've been like 'naw! I don't want company right now'."

"That's something you'd never have to ask. Mí casá es sú casá." He reassures her. "How she holding up?"

"So far she's been taking it one day at a time." Remembering she needed to call and check up on her. "I know she's made several attempts to contact Arnez and talk the situation over with him. But, he hasn't answered for her yet." Feeling sorry for her friend. Still baffled about how her and Mario ended up together again.

"He'll come around eventually." Picking up the remote off the table. "He really cared about her." Pushing the power button. "We men take betrayal a bit more serious then women." Flipping through the channels. Trying to see what he could find. "Just give him some time. He'll pop up eventually. If he doesn't. Then, she has to deal with the consequences of her actions." Having no remorse.

"You ain't got to be so harsh about it."

"I ain't being harsh. I'm just keeping it real." Ignoring her accusations.

"But, he'd come around. I know he will." Still flipping threw the channels. "I need to get up and get myself together."

"Where you going?"

"We got practice today." He replied. Laying the remote back on the coffee table.

"Oh, I forgot about that."

"Look at ya. Always trying to keep tabs on somebody."

"Ya darn skippy!"

Bernard arose from the couch and made his exit to go get dressed for practice. Leaving Shelly sitting in the living room by herself. Picking up the remote to turn the television completely off. Shelly relaxed on the love seat and contemplated on her next move. In the mist of thinking, she thought about her dear friend and grew more concerned about her then she was before. Shelly and Jasmine had been through a lot with one another every since the beginning of their friendship. And it seemed as if, once they've crossed one hurdle another would follow. Not knowing if it's their luck that's running low, or if it's just the trials they have to overcome. One thing for sure, Shelly was ready to walk down easy street and she felt going to another city would surely be the turn of a new leaf.

"Well mama, I'm headed to practice!" Bernard yelled down the hall. Ring! Ring! Ring! "Could you answer that for me bay and take a message for me please!" Slamming the door.

Ring! Ring! Ring!..... Ring! Ring! Ring!......

"Hello."

"Hi, may I speak with Bernard?"

"He's not here. Would you like to leave a message?"

"Naw, I'll call back." The unknown caller said with an attitude.

"Is this Shelly?" She continued to pry.

"This is she." Caught off guard. Shelly proceeded to answer. "And may I ask with whom am I speaking with?" Curious of who could have known her identity since she'd just moved in. *I wonder who this could be and how they know my name? It can't be one of his family members because they wouldn't call private. And, why she got an attitude? This bitch.* Entertaining her subconscious thoughts.

"If you're not clear on who I am. I'm Bernard's ex-girlfriend who you called maybe eight to seven months ago accusing me of messing with him. Even though, I told you I wasn't." Ranting in the phone as she motioned her right hand back and forth. Like she was in a confrontation. "Umm yeah, because of that little stunt you pulled. I noticed Bernard may have not forewarned you of who I am." Talking smack as if she was the baddest thing smoking.

I can care less about who this bitch think she is. Shelly thought to herself as she glanced at the phone with a smug look on her face, before she placed it back to her ear.

"Well…. Since that night, because you pissed me off. I started back hanging with him."

Pissed you off! Appalled by her verbiage. *I like her nerve….* Still debating with her thoughts as this anonymous caller continues to annoy.

"And we've been sexing and hanging out ever since. Just to let you know." Laying the icing on the cake.

They've been what! Considering hanging up in this callers face.

"He actually got angry." Pausing as she laughed. "Because I didn't come over on his birthday." Still giggling in the background. "Oh… And I was with him Valentine's Day as well….." Feeling there wasn't any competition concerning Mr. Curry.

I wonder how he found time to squeeze that in, because he was with me both times as well.

"Umm… Let me see. I spend the night every Monday and Wednesday. Therefore, I know when you're calling the next following Tuesday or whenever he doesn't answer."

That son of a bitch. Shelly gasp for air.

"I'll take the blame." Trying to be modest. "That's because he's with me." Thinking of more beans to spill. "We went out last Saturday. If you don't believe me; you can view my mobile pictures and you'll see him having fun at Destiny Mill."

She still carrying on. Shelly thought as she grew tired of hearing this grand confession.

"I spent the night this past Tuesday. Naturally we fucked. And I'm supposed to spend the day with him tomorrow."

Groupie… Shaking her head in disbelief. Thinking on how pathetic this girl really is.

"We supposed to be going to the laundry mat and later to the Comedy Club. But, being I'm getting bored. You can have your boyfriend back." Giving Shelly permission to clam her leftovers. "And by the way, I'm expecting."

"Expecting what?" Shelly couldn't believe the words she was hearing.

"Don't act, you know what it means. And that meeting he had in Vermont, that's a negative sweetie pie. He was in the Camions with me." Chuckling as she gave Shelly the business.

"Oh no this bitch didn't."

With all the drama that went down this past week, Shelly never would've guessed Bernard could've dropped the ball on her like this. *Then again, the signs were always there.* But, she thought she was being insecure and didn't want to seem like 'that chick' that didn't trust her man. All of the calls and receiving no responses to text messages she sent to tell him she missed him. Were now making since. *And got the nerve to try and lie.* It was as if everything he had been doing had flashed before her as she held the phone in disbelief.

"Why are you telling me this now?" Mad, but unsure of her feelings.

"Because I want my family to work and I know the only thing standing in the way of us, is 'you'." You could hear her attitude in the way she said it.

Renee hated Shelly. She hated her with a passion and never even met her a day in her life. All she knew, this was the woman standing in the way of her bills getting paid. And if removed, she could have it all.

And got the nerve to try and make Jazz's situation nothing major. He got some nerve.

"Well, I'm sorry to hear that. And I'm sorry you put yourself threw all this trouble to contact me." Taking control of the conversation. "Telling me this because…." Prolonging the inevitable. So Renee will know she's not concerned about her or the child she's claiming to be Bernard's. "You thought you were going to gain something from it. Ha!" She laughed. "You need to come out of that little bubble he got you living in sweetie. Because you're seriously delusional if you think I'm going to let you walk off with my man." Seeing how naive this so called Renee was. "I call it a bubble because no one knows about you. He has you completely isolated from the rest of the people in his life." Making sure her point was being delivered clear enough so she could understand what she meant. "If you were relevant, he'd flaunt you. And at least one soul outside of you two would recognize you."

Trick.

"You claiming y'all taking trips together, but he refers to them as business." She continued. "Please help me understand the thoughts of a sideline. Cause I can't be one, if they think and act like you." She questioned. "That's real shit."

"What he tells you ain't got nothing to do with me or our child."

I just know she ain't trying to tell me off. She better act like she know and stop while she's ahead.

"He say what he has to. To make sure, you don't bring that drama to my door step."

I can see that. But he slipped somewhere down the line because she calling my phone.

"Yeah, I know about you."

"Is that right?"

"I surely do. And you're sadly mistaken if you think I'm going to let you continue to be a factor in his life when this baby arrives."

"Whatever bitch. You sound stupid." Shaking her head in disgust. "With that being said Mrs. Insignificant. I'm going to say this one time and one time only. And I hope I've made myself clear to you by the time I've finished my sentence." She bullied.

"Anything that comes out of your mouth is irrelevant to me."

"Bernard is my man."

"And he's my babies father, your point?"

"And ain't no money grubbing, turkey basting, want to be a family, delusional ass groupie. About to come up in here and fuck up some shit that I invested my time in that I can't get back."

"It ain't my fault time sagging on them titties and he want something a bit more youthful."

"Just because she desperate enough and greedy enough to get pregnant by a nigga that ain't even man enough and won't man up. To admit he's been seeing on the side. Where I'm from, we call those 'sidelines'. My bad, I left out ho. Take heed to the warning I'm giving and hear me well. That bastard child you claim to be his. Better turn up to be, when the results come back. Because if it says 'negative', bitch it's going to be me and you. And ain't no monkey going to be able to stop that show." She said in a calm but assertive way so Renee could tell this wasn't a game she was playing. *This shit just got real.* Shelly said to herself as she placed the telephone back down on the receiver. *So he been doing big things I see.* "Bet."

Shelly packed all her belongings she brought with her over Bernard's house. Shocked, because she found out her man had been cheating. She couldn't wait to get home and tell Jazz every detail of what took place. Speaking of her Jazzy poo. Shelly hoped by giving her space, she had pulled her emotions together within that time. Even if she hadn't, she at least needed to be available to listen to her problems now. Arriving at the house, Shelly grab all her luggage and hauled it in the front door. *I hope this child is woke at least.* She didn't call to warn her that she was coming home because she was to frustrated to call. She wanted to deliver the message in person.

"Jazzy!" Shelly sung through the front corridor as she walked in the house. Using her foot to shut the door behind her. *I don't need no bugs flying around in here. Especially since I've ran out of bug spray and ain't went to the store yet.* "How you feeling lady?" She asked. Receiving no response as she continued to sing Jasmines name. "Jazzy….. You know you hear me calling you girl!" She yelled as she searched room from room. Anxious to spill her guts. "I know you in here!" Feeling as if Jasmine was ignoring her. "You better not still be in here crying woman. I need you to have pulled your shit together honey and started working on some master plan in regard to winning Arnez back." Attempting to make light of the situation. "And you wouldn't believe the call I got this morning honey." Scurrying room from room. "A bitch stepped out her lane on me this morning. Straight disrespecting! Had the nerve to tell me she had been sleeping with Nard! And that ain't even half the mess she was saying!" Opening the blinds in every room she entered. "Woman if you don't answer me! And, why you got this house all closed up? You could've at least cracked the windows! It stank in here!" She shouted until she found her sitting in the same spot she was in when she was last there. Still Jasmine said nothing as she sat in the chair. "Trick! You know you hear me!" Now furious as she made her way around the couch to see why Jasmine wasn't answering her. "JASMINE!!"

As tears welled in her eyes. Shelly screamed hysterically at the sight of her dear friend lifeless body crouched in her recliner. With such force that she was unable to catch her breath. Shelly was having a panic attack for the first time in her life. Over whelmed, she continued to yell out.

"Why did you do this?" She yelled. Bending down to rock Jasmines cold body in her arms. "I should've been here for you to tell you everything was going to be okay. I never should've been so hard on you." Taking the blame. "I knew you were hurt from what happened. But, I didn't know it was this deep mama." She cried. "I should've stayed." Feeling the fault was hers. Thinking if she wasn't so caught up on Bernard, her friend would still be alive. "I should have stayed!" Crying out as she continued to rock. "Wake up!" Demanding Jasmine to open her eyes as she shook violently.

"How could you leave me like this?" Clinching down on Jasmines shoulders. Crying as she hugged her. "Why didn't you call me?" Pulling away to stare her in her face. Waiting on a response. "You could've called and told me you needed me." Caressing her hair to lay the straggly strings flat with the rest of her ponytail. "I would've came back!" Dropping a steam of tears on Jasmine cheeks. "I would have came back for you!" Rocking uncontrollably. "I would've stayed and listened. You were my sister. My best friend. We could have fixed this." Still unable to get a grip on the tears. "You didn't have to do this! I need you. What am I going to do now, huh?" Thinking of herself selfishly. Hoping this was all a nightmare and she would awake shortly after.

With the unexpected drama continuing to unfold. Shelly would've never assumed Jasmine would commit suicide. She was literally in a state of disbelief. And, insecure of how to handle everything by herself. Glancing around the room, she noticed Jasmine had been drinking. By the empty bottles that were scattered in the floor.

"I can't believe you did this! Have you even fed yourself since I left?" She fussed. "Look at what you've went and done to yourself!" Feeling a slight headache coming from the constant crying. "Why Jazz? Why!" Hitting her as she continued to seek a response. "HELP!" She screamed. "Somebody HELP ME!!" Yelling out with enough force, which caused her to scratch her throat. "PLEASE! HELP ME!!!" One of the neighbors overheard the screams and dialed for the authorities. "I can't believe you did this! Who am I going to discuss my issues with? I can't believe this is happening!" She cried. When Shelly looked up, she saw a note on the coffee table. Hearing the sirens drawing near, she stuffed the note in her pocket.

Carefully laying Jasmines body flat on the floor. Shelly got up and walked outside to direct the police to her home. Standing at the edge of her porch, she waved her arms in the air so they could see her. With the loud sirens sounding from the ambulance and the police vehicles. All of her neighbors that were home at the time, came out to see what all the commotion was about. As one of the police patrol cruisers pulled at the end of her driveway. Shelly stepped down to meet the officer in the middle.

"What's the emergency ma'am?" He asked as the ambulance pulled beside his vehicle.

"I came home to check on her and I found her like this." Shelly explained.

"How long have you been gone?" Looking Shelly in her eyes as he awaited her response. Wondering if she could've killed the victim and was attempting to pass it off as a suicide.

"Well, I left her here for a couple days so she could get herself together, but it never crossed my mind she would do something like this."

"Has she ever been suicidal or attempted to take her own life before?"

"No, not that I know of. She was mentally stable as I."

"Well, could you tell me as much as possible about what could have led her to decide this as her fate?" Placing his hands on his hips, with a puzzling look on his face.

"To be honest officer, I have no idea." She admitted. Staring blankly back at him.. "To my understanding she was heart broken over a recent break up. But, she's been in and out of relationships before." Scratching her head. "I don't see how this one is any different."

"If we need to call you to come down to the station for more questioning. Would you be willing to come?" Writing down her statement in his mini note pad. As she gave an account of her where about at the time of the incident.

"Of course, whatever you need."

"Being you are the only witness in this case. We need to make sure we have all the details of what could have possibly pushed her to such a tragic end."

"I understand."

While the Med team rolled her friend body away. Shelly stood in a daze, watching until she couldn't see the ambulance anymore. Picking up her phone, she started dialing Jasmines mother and her own family to inform them of her current situation. She thought to call Arnez, but she knew this was something he deserved to hear face to face. Since he's at the club most of the day. Shelly got in her truck and made her way over there. When she pulled up, Rock was outside setting up the ropes to start the line. The club was still closed at the time. He was just getting an early start on the opening preparations.

"Hey Shell." He greeted. "Are you ok?" Noticing the paleness of her face.

"Is Arnez here?"

"Yeah, he's in the office. Is everything alright?" He asked again as her eyes started to flood.

"No, but I really need to speak with him right away." She urged.

"You know you're always welcome here. If it's anything you need that I can help you with. Don't be afraid to speak up about it, ok."

"Thanks, I really appreciate that. I'll remember that for next time."

"No problem. And whatever it is that's bothering you. Everything will turn out just fine. I'm sure of it." But Shelly didn't reply. She just walked passed him as if he said nothing. With her head hung low and her arm clutching her bag. Regretting the idea of not wearing shades.

Arnez was siting at his desk going over the financials from the previous night, when he heard a knock at the door. Shuffling all the receipts, he placed them in a small drawer underneath the desk. Arnez was nice but he didn't like people in his personal business when it came to his money. And with the employees he had. Not saying he didn't trust them. His past made him trust no one, not even family. When money was involved.

"Come in!" He yelled.

She slowly opened the door trying to figure the best way to tell him what happened. When she stepped in, he couldn't see her face because she had her back faced him as she closed the door.

"Hey Shell, I didn't expect to see you today. How can I help you hot shot?"

As she turned to face him. He could see the hurt in her eyes as she looked him deep in his.

"Is everything alright?" He asked. For he pitied her, because he could sense whatever ailed her. Was something truly heavy and he wanted to be as supportive as he could. "What's wrong?" Giving her his undivided attention. "All you have to do is tell me. No matter what it is and I'd help you no questions asked." He continued to reassure her as he arose from his chair to go and console his business partner.

Thinking it was nothing more then a minor set back with the business or some small mishap between her and Bernard. He started asking more questions to show his support.

"Is everything ok down at the shop? Is production still flowing the way it's supposed to?" Pacing around the room with his hands behind his back. Preparing himself for any possible solutions he may have to think up instantaneously. "I haven't received any negative reviews from Kelly. Therefore, my gut is leading me in a different direction." He continued to pace. "Are your sisters' okay?" Still trying to guess what could be ailing her. "Did you and Nard have a disagreement? If so, things will get better. Just give it a couple days and it will work itself out." Standing with a confused look on his face waiting on Shelly to tell him what's going on. Nothing could have ever prepared him for the words that were about to come out of her mouth.

"She's dead!" A distraught Shelly blurted out.

"Who's dead?" He questioned with a look of uncertainty as his heart sank to the pit of his stomach. At the thought of the name he was anticipating her to say.

"Jasmine!" She welled. "She slit her wrists in my living room." Crying hysterically. "I found her when I went back home today." Unable to keep her body balanced. With her legs feeling as if they were about to give out on her. "She was just laying there Arnez." Letting go of her upper body strength. "I don't know how long she was like that or what made her do it. All I know is my sister gone." Swinging her arms lifelessly back and forth. "My baby is gone and I have no way of bringing her back. I have no way of convincing myself this isn't real. She's gone Arnez!"

Lost for words Arnez flopped down in his chair. Confused, hurt, and heart broken. He didn't know what to say or think. He was so distraught by the news. He didn't have enough strength to look up at Shelly, who was sliding slowly down the wall.

"Why?" Directing his question to no one in particular. As he covered his face with his hands. To hide his tears in the darkness they created.

For the first time in six years Arnez wept. He had so much pain, so much anger, hidden in the depths of his heart. That this final test was the last straw. He couldn't hold it in no longer. Being as secretive as he was, he never discussed his past life with any of his new friends. Because he thought he'd left his past behind him. But now it feels as if his past has came back to haunt him. Using this tragedy as his karma. The woman he loved not only defiled his bed, but she took her life as well. A blast from the past, he thought. With a twist. Emotions were beyond control in this small corner office at 'The Spot'.

"Why! Why would she do something as stupid as this?" Tossing everything he had on top of his desk on the floor. Every piece of paper even down to his laptop were all victims of Arnezes wrath. "Did it ever cross her mind that she couldn't come back from this? Is she that damn selfish that she would make a decision and not consider the people that loved her!" Slamming his fists down in the desk. "I can't believe this!"

"That's what I keep asking myself."

"How can she be so selfish?" He asked. Hoping for an explanation that could justify why. "How could she do this to me, to us? I loved her!

No, I love her!" Falling to his knees as he cried out for the woman he loved. "Deciding the best thing she could've done to better our situation, was to hurt me more. By taking the easy way out!" Pouring his true feelings out to Shelly. "I'm the hurt one here, not her!" Angry at the thought of her leaving his life in shambles. "We could've worked things out! All I needed was some space. Is that to much to ask for? Get a grip on what I was doing wrong that could have caused her to do what she did to us. Was I working too much?" Questioning himself as a man. "Was I not spending enough time or giving her enough attention. I planned on coming back to her. Just to listen to her side of the story. I know I over reacted, but." Beating himself up. "What did she expect me to do? What did she expect me to think?" He asked.

Reaching into her pocket. Shelly pulled out the note she found on her coffee table.

"I haven't read it yet." She informed him. "I found it laying on my table. So I grabbed it before any of the policeman could see it and take it in for observation." As she handed it to him. She reassured him that she would keep him posted on the details of the funeral.

"How could she?" He cried.

WOW

After a few months had passed. Shelly decided to give Jasmine a call. Since she changed her number a few weeks back, she had to reach her via email. Contemplating if this was something she really wanted to do, because she knew it could back fire. Jasmine could act like the child she was and not respond, or even try and dis her attempt to mend their friendship. Either way, Shelly wanted to repair what they once had. This was the longest she and her best friend went without speaking and she didn't want the silence to go any further.

"Are you still mad?" She asked.

"I stopped caring." Jasmines emailed back.

"Oh."

"You have your own insecurities about me. Therefore, we will never see eye to eye. But know while you was shittin' on me I was a damn good friend to you still." Jasmine argued. "No details, know that."

"I never shitted on you! I've always been there for you when you needed me." Taking offence to Jasmines accusations.

Shelly couldn't believe the things Jasmine was accusing her of. She thought she was a good friend. At least she was to the best of her ability.

She felt she treated her the way she wanted to be treated. With respect, loyalty, support, and dependability. But, people don't appreciate those values as she did anymore. So she thought.

"As a matter of fact. I was the only one there and willing to put up with all the B.S you seemed to get us involved in." Directing her attacks to their previous run ins they'd experienced together. "Between you needing money and that crazy ass Mario. You should be happy someone was there for your ass! If it was anybody else, they would've been cut your ignorant ass off! But, I stayed down! I stayed down because that's what friends do!" Typing aggressively on the keyboard. "Your problem is you never understand a girl needed space." Tilting her head back for air to calm her nerves. "It became overwhelming for me. The constant calling, the frequent arguing, and the extra drama you dragged me in with your relationship. I needed my freaking space! So I took it! That don't mean I'm cutting you off, I just wanted to be alone for a while. Nothing personal."

"Girl stop it I say!" Jasmine chuckled. "Save them lies for somebody else. You didn't even want to give me your new number, but to each it's on." Acting nonchalant like what Shelly was saying didn't mean anything to her. "Nevertheless, know I'm still a good friend to you and I don't even fuck with you. It's deeper than you'll ever know!"

"Because I knew you'd be calling me at six in the freaking morning, waking me up out my freaking sleep, with some nonsense! So yeah, I ignored you for a minute!" *She got her nerve.* "You don't respect me during my hours of sleep! Just because you woke, don't mean everyone else is. And on top of that, another thing that bothered me about you. Ever since I got that car. If you needed me I was there, no questions asked. If I could be there for you, I was. And ever since day one, not once did you ever fix your mouth to offer me a drop of gas! Not once!" Fumbling through the key board. "Every time I step foot in your car or even your aunts. I always gave at least five dollars every time you asked me to put in on gas!"

Jasmine Continued to read. The way she saw it, Shelly was full of shit. What friend leaves you in your time of need? Yeah, Shelly made a few valid points about the Mario situation. But, Jasmine was to self-centered to ever admit any wrong. By Shelly being her best friend so she called herself. She was supposed to be at Jasmine's disposal whenever she needed her.

I know this bitch ain't trying to find a real reason to be mad. Hell if she wanted some gas money, all she had to do was ask. Ain't nobody going to just offer the shit freely. Closed mouths don't get fed around this camp. And I ain't volunteering shit! Fuck that!

"Last time I talked to you. What you do?" Acknowledging the elephant in the room. "Over a period of time I started feeling like you were using me." She admitted. "Every time I called, even though it was the same boring shit. Same mistakes, I needed you to listen and you couldn't even do that." Continuing to take her anger out on the keys. "You'd down play what I had to say and start talking about your issues. Not once did I ever complain!"

"Well, hell. If she felt like this she should've said something." Jasmine blurted out as she read.

"I've listened and put my feelings on the back burner. I've tried to help you better yourself and suggest things I thought you could benefit from. And soon as you get motivated, you back track and start fucking with those bomb ass friends that's always fucking you over!!!!" Feeling her pressure starting to rise from the anger she had let build up and was now releasing. "And when the damage was done I was the one there to help you get back on your feet! YOU WERE NOT A GOOD FRIEND TO ME JASMINE! I never asked you for NOTHING! All I asked was for you to listen when I needed someone there to vent to!"

"You called me plenty of times waking me up out my sleep!" Jasmine retaliated. "Crying in my ear! Do miss me with the fuckery!" Growing tired of Shelly's complaints. "The other shit is irrelevant and a thing of the pass. Enjoy your day. When I write you in a few years and include you in on details of what's going on. You gone feel real dumb! But like I said, to each it's on." Send… "Going back and forth is petty and I can be real rude and end this convo, but I'm going to be the bigger person here. Plus, I had my own issues and they deeper then you can imagine. You couldn't relate."

She always hollering about her issues being bigger then somebody else's. She don't know what people got going on. Shelly thought as she continued to read.

"And you a fucking idiot if you felt I was using you! I'm the one person believe it or not that didn't. And for you to say I wasn't a good friend! Then why the fuck you emailing me then? I am your best friend! Because I could've fucked you over big time, know that!"

"Well how else would you have expected me to feel when I finally grow up and started seeing everyone who claimed to be a friend and or family member was using me. I analyzed everyone and in the end that's how I felt. Cause that's what it started appearing to me as." Send… "So I'll be that idiot!"

"I know and you'll be apologizing later."

"YOU WEREN'T THERE WHEN I NEEDED YOU!!!!!!!! We always disagree and take breaks. This time was no different from the others. I needed your support and you weren't there! The bad part about it is the fact that we weren't even on bad terms that time Jasmine!"

"You supposed to be my best friend and you didn't even know I was suffering depression! Talking to doctors and everything! But you don't even know what the fuck I'm addressing for you not to call me a good friend. Believe you're an idiot, have better judgment of character. But understand, I was never against you. If you were someone else I'd be giving you the business shawty, but your feelings to delicate. But you in the dark because what I want to say I know it'll break you down. I'll tell you but it won't be today."

"If you my BEST FRIEND, you supposed to have told me that! I told you everything! I was depressed as well, I even thought about suicide plenty of nights! The only reason I never did it because I didn't want to go to hell for the shit!"

"Like I said. I know you and for you to think I'm a fucked up friend, you don't even know the half."

What the heck is she keep talking about.

"But trust you're going to feel real dumb!"

Yeah, I feel dumb cause you keep saying the same shit over and over, that's why.

"And you so simple minded you don't even know how to read in-between the lines. I'm done with this convo. Almost everything been said. You need time to grow up and when you do, I'm going to enlighten your ass on a few things. Enjoy life."

"Just because I smile doesn't mean that's how I feel on the inside. I've learned how to hide certain emotions and transfer them to something that won't make since to be hurt over. 'Relationships' but ok, whatever."

"I was a friend to you when we weren't even cool. One day Bernard wrote me through email and asked me out for drinks."

Shelly's heart sank before Jasmine could finish her statement. For she couldn't believe out of all people, Bernard would stoop so low as to approach her best friend. Lost for words this was the first time Shelly had ever been speechless. Of all the thoughts roaming in her head. She had to force herself to refocus back on what Jasmine had to say. It felt as if someone had punched her smack dab in the middle of her stomach and she was struggling to catch her next breath.

"I declined, and he let me know he didn't smoke anymore."

Now I know this is recent because he just stopped maybe a couple months ago. So I know she's telling the truth.

"I was broke. Therefore, I used him for what I could and he brought me some weed as well. I did talk about you, but it was out of anger. But I didn't fuck him. You know that's not my style."

Yeah right. Shelly thought to herself. But she knew differently. Jasmine was notorious for being scandalous. Especially when a man was involved. *That's what you're saying now.*

"If she went over his house. Something had to go down." She said to herself. "Because it's not like Jazz to turn down sex, if offered. And knowing Bernard; it was offered and she took it."

"He pulled out a stack trying to show me he got a lil check." Shelly continued to read. "But I used him for some weed, that's it."

Hoes…

"I told you he ain't shit."

"So now he ain't shit! But you wasn't saying that when you were with him!" Yelling at the computer. Unsure if she should be angry or hurt from the news she's receiving.

"Just because I'm telling you this, don't mean go crazy and start blowing his phone up." Jasmine advised.

You should've thought about that before you opened up your mouth.

"Bottom line he ain't shit, so move on. You see how niggas do."

I see how bitches do! You ain't no better then him. Shaking her head. *While you trying to make him the criminal.*

"Thanks for telling me." Expressing gratitude to confuse Jasmine on what she really felt. "The irony in the matter is, I ain't even hurt." Maintaining her poker face demeanor. "It is what it is, I guess." *Trifflin bitch.* "I'm happy you used him. At least somebody benefited out the situation.

You should've got some money off him." She edged on. "That's fucked up that he would do it like that though. But, what can I say. No love lost."

Remembering Jasmine stating she was talking about her. Shelly wanted to know if he said anything negative as well. Curiosity kills the cat every time. Good thing they claim to have seven lives.

"Did he ever bad talk me?" Sweating as she refreshed her browser as if it would speed up the delivery of the mail in her inbox.

"Shelly, I'm always going to be here for you." She said in efforts to change the subject.

That ain't what I asked her.

"We best friends. People know you have a great heart and you real giving."

She just saying this cause she feel guilty and trying to reconcile.

"I didn't know full details but I knew enough. I still hate Bernard, but I got him back."

It sounds to me like he used her and played her. Got them drawls and sent her on her way.

"Ha haaaa." Shelly chuckled.

"He burnt up all his gas, searching for me some weed." She boasted.

This don't even sound like something Nard would do.

"I love you Jasmine." Shelly emailed back. Even though, she never admitted how hurt she really was from what Jasmine had done.

"So yea, I'm your best friend." She continued to babble. "I asked him about Nichole."

Shelly gasps for air at the thought of another dear friend stabbing her in the back over a man. Apart of her can expect this from Jasmine, but Niko. Shelly couldn't fathom the betrayal.

"He said he never fucked with her."

Wheew. Taking a deep breath to relieve herself of the sudden anxiety she experienced. *Yeah, because Niko ain't nasty or trifling like you.*

"I just played it cool." She continued. "We sat on the same couch, but different ends."

If they sat on two different ends. Then, why she going in so much detail about it. Trying to get that lie down pack.

"I don't play that shit. But, that's what I was hinting at. That's why I was so mad when you said what you said but it's water under the bridge now."

"What did I say?" Trying to figure out what she's rambling about. *And this trick still ain't answered my question.*

"But, if I knew what I know now. I should've went harder and got his boney ass robbed."

Shelly gave one last genuine laugh as she continued to read her emails as they continued to flow.

"God works in mysterious ways honey. Maybe it was best that I didn't know, because I probably would've been to mad with you. Just to let you know. I wouldn't have bailed you out either." Making sure she typed her last statement clear enough that her point would be understood.

"I wouldn't have got caught. They could've robbed him and I wouldn't have asked for shit. I would've been satisfied knowing he got punk'd."

What she feeling a certain type of way for. That's how I know she's not telling the whole truth. He couldn't stand her so he said. But I know how niggas lie. When they say they don't like you, they do. And when they say they like you, they like you. So it really don't matter what they say. It's all for the booty anyway.

"But yeah, God do. I'm just vengeful." She admitted. "God knew what my mind was on, and you know I'm a strong believer of karma."

"Ha!" Shelly blurted.

"It all comes back and he's going to feel it."

It surely does. Agreeing subconsciously.

"So, with that being said. You can't trust no nigga. We been knew we could do better. Both of us deserve better."

Hell I can't trust you! Real friends regardless the situation wouldn't have any ties to another friends ex. Defiantly, when they've been dating as long as me and Nard have. But that's neither here nor there. What's done is done. And what you do in the dark will come to the light. But, I figure her guilt is what caused her to confess. A guilty conscience is the key to restless nights.

"With all the shit I've been through with Bernard. I'm surprise I'm still able to forgive and allow another man in. It ain't easy on him though. I kind of feel bad but not really." Revealing she had a new found love. Leaning over to turn up her radio. Which at the time, was playing 'what if a woman' by one of her favorite male artist.

"What he eat don't make you shit. Fuck him! He don't have no remorse nor sympathy for what he did to you. I don't see him coming and apologizing to you. If I never said anything, you would've never known."

Shit neither do you! Getting roused up again. *Just because this bitch confessed, don't mean shit! I hope she don't think this means we will be buddy, buddy again. And go skipping off into the sunset holding hands. Cause she got another thing coming if she thought that.*

"And he's going to have a hard life. Starting with that bastard child he got on the way. Sorry, but it's real. I'm a strong believer that God put people in your life for a reason. Like I've always told you, be patient and your man will come. You got to go through bullshit to see the light and know how to react. And, how to learn from your mistakes. So you won't make them again. Everyone can't be trusted and everyone doesn't deserve you."

"You don't have to apologize to me." Shelly told her. "No apologies needed." Even though, Shelly was playing it cool. She still was thinking she couldn't even trust her own best friend. The one person in the whole wide world that she was supposed to be able to.

SINCERELY

Dear Arnez,

Bay, I love you so much. So much, you will never know how deep my love goes for you. And could never understand the pain I feel for hurting you the way I did, or by the way I'm doing now. Or, the agony I feel at this moment as I write my last words to you. With every tear that falls while the point of my pen slides across this sheet of paper. I swear on my love for you, I never intentionally wanted to hurt you in this type or any type of way papa.

You were, you are, and will forever be the beat in my heart and the yearning in my soul. My eye twinkle every time I see your face and I feel loneliness every time you leave my space. It never crossed my mind that I would ever see the day where I would betray your trust and us the way I did. Not only your trust, but jeopardize what we built with one another for someone so insignificant as Mario. But names shouldn't matter.

I loved you from the first day I laid eyes on you, and I love you still. I knew I wanted to be your wife and give you all the babies you agreed that we could create together. Just as soon as you let me know you wanted it with me to. I lived to wake up to you and put a smile on your face, and died to fall asleep next to you. Because you were the light of my life. No one could ever replace the space you have in my heart.

171

You are my everything and believe, please believe. My heart is crying out for you right now to come rescue me from this pain I feel. I know I never said it enough but that's how I truly feel. I want to apologize for always trying to hold back my love for you. And for those days I acted like I couldn't tell you how I felt. Even though, I was dying on the inside to jump on you and smother you with all the kisses you'd allow me to give.

I only did it because I was afraid if I told you everything. You would hurt me, but we see who really was the bad guy. And now I'm wishing I said it more then instead of now, which is later. I never planned any of this or ever attempted to hurt you in any way. I really would like for you to know I was not having an affair on you and never have I in the course of our relationship. It just happened that one time. I swear it just happened. You were enough. But, I allowed myself to fall victim to lust.

That day you left for work. Mario popped up literally at our front door and told me he had been stalking me. I know it sounds crazy for me to say a guy that was stalking me ended up getting caught in our bed. Trust me, I've played this over and over in my head. Trying to figure how I could make this not sound the way it does. But, the truth must be told. I have no explanation on how to make this make since to you. Or help you understand the reason I did what I did. But you shouldn't have to, because I was wrong.

Now that I've said it aloud to myself. I can't even justify what I did to me either. I was stupid and I sound stupid. I don't know what I was thinking. I wasn't thinking. If I could take it back I would. I try to live my life with no regrets, but I guess there's a first time for everything. But, everyone says that when they know they've messed up. Honestly, if I were still in that moment and I had to decide. I know I still would've done it. Not because of you or anything that you've done. It has nothing to do with you. You have been nothing but perfect to me. That's coming from my heart.

I guess I'm weak without reason when it comes to that man. And that's a flaw I could never erase no matter how many times I've tried. Apart of my selfishness, I admit. But that still doesn't justify my actions and I'm not trying to. One thing I know for certain I DO NOT LOVE HIM. It was physical. I am and will forever be very much in love with Arnez Jenkins until death do us part. Yet I find irony in that last statement. Wherefore, I bit my own tongue with it.

I know you may be confused on why I decided to do what I'm doing. So to give you peace. I'm going to use these last four minutes to explain. A couple years ago after me and Mario split, he started dating and having sex with random women recklessly. I knew it and everyone else knew about him and his late nights as well. He started partaking in these random acts while we were still together. Which was one of the reasons we split in the first place, among others. You see.

In the mist of his endeavors, he contracted the HIV virus. I knew this, but it never crossed my mind that night he came over. Everyone knew about it, but no one knew for certain. As if it was just a rumor because of his ho-ish ways. Once I embraced him, I remembered. But, it was too late. He had already penetrated me without a condom. It shames me to admit to have done something so irresponsible as to not use protection. And it never dawned on me that he just got released from his prison sentence either.

I know you maybe questioning if I knew, why did I still do it? That's a question I can't answer. Because the more and more I try to rationalize it with myself, the more I drank. One of those 'what were you thinking' moments. But you say fuck it, it's in there now. At the time it happened for the life of me the thought never came up. It was as if I never knew because I couldn't remember. I really feel as if this is Gods way of punishing me papa, I swear I feel it is. And as my fate is sealed. The contents of this bottle, helps ease the thought of where I will spend eternity. It's not a good place, but these last sips are helping me cope. Ain't shit else I can do.

When you put me out. I knew you may have needed some time to think things through, but I knew we could never be together again. One mistake has scared me for life, and I can't live the rest of my days like this. The children I've always dreamed of will never become a reality. Because they would be born with it even if we always used condoms or got artificially in simulated. I can't do that to them, and I wouldn't do that to them. I can't bear putting you through it either. You don't deserve this. I can't continue on knowing I could never really feel you inside of me any longer. The thought of our skins never touching. Would be the death of me over time. Because that's how I feel your love. Arnez I love you with all my soul. I really felt you were created for me. When you were born, everything was right in the world. Because you truly are a gem.

Don't ever fault yourself or wish things could be different, because it's not and you can't. You could never do no wrong in my eyes baby. You've been nothing but good to me since the first day we became an item baby and I will never forget that. I wanted a life that wasn't in the plan for me. And I held on to false hope because I believed and knew you would give it to me. But most days I felt as if I didn't deserve you or it.

You can't turn a 'ho' into a 'housewife'. No matter if you take her out the hood and give her a new identity. She will always resort back to the woman that's on the inside. And that's just who I was before I met you. Please tell Shell I love her and she will always be the best friend I could've ever prayed for in a lifetime. There is no replacing her and I don't know what I would've done if I didn't have her in my life. She really is a saint. But I know she's going to be just fine. I LOVE YOU ARNEZ JENKINS AND I AM DEEPLY SORRY MY LOVE.

Sincerely,

Jazzy Poo

AIN'T THAT A BITCH

It's been six months since Jasmine's death, and Shelly still have her days when she wishes she could call her up and tell her everything that's going on under the sun. Since the burial. Shelly had been living with Bernard. She couldn't fathom staying in the house her friend died in. She couldn't even keep her composure when she went back to go gather her things, because it was such a struggle for her. She had to hire a moving company to come over to pack, load, and ship her belongings to her. Living with Bernard was a sight to see, because every morning he would awake and expect breakfast and there was none. He would sway around the house as if everything was ok and Shelly would curse him out in her mind. But, he still thinks she doesn't know anything about the baby he had on the way with Renee. With Shelly being secretive and Renee trying to savor every second Bernard spent with her. Neither of them were ever going to spill the beans that soon. Within those months, because Bernard had been staying out late and claiming to always be at practice. Shelly had been secretly taking the money he had been giving her to go shopping with and stashing it away for the day she planned on leaving.

"It hasn't been the same without you mama." Shelly stated to herself while leaning up against the island in the middle of the kitchen floor. Reminiscing on her past life with a friend that could never be replaced.

"I miss you so much."

Since the economy started failing financially. The clothing line she had started to loose some of it's revenue. Therefore, Shine wasn't selling as well as it did when she first launched it. Plus, with all the medical expenses accumulating for Nette. Most of her income she had been receiving had been tangled in a web. Looking over several papers trying to figure out her next move, Shelly receives a text. **"It's his bitch!"** With a photo copy of the results attached as a picture message.

"How did this bitch even get my cell number?" She asked. "Whelp, I guess that means it's about that time."

Since Bernard told Shelly he was going to practice, she already knew what time it was. Cleverly, she hired a detective to follow him. How did she compensate this production you ask? With his money. How ironic is that. Now ain't that a stick in the mud. Therefore, when he says 'practice' that means he's going over her house. He doesn't have the slightest idea Shelly knows he doesn't have practice Tuesday and Thursdays. Yet, today just happened to be Thursday. Putting her sweats and sneakers on, she rushed for the door. Shelly sped to Renee's house. Address courtesy of the investigator. And she didn't bother texting back or calling.

"The same way this bitch can get my number and call me, is the same way I can come up with an address to track that ass down." She boasted.

Because she was so amp, she had to play a little aggressive music to make sure she stayed that way. No one wants to be angry with someone and when they finally get to the person. Loose the urge to kick their ass. Shelly stopped paying the crew to follow Bernard once she got the information she needed. Therefore, she knew where to go. Because they showed her the house before the contract ended for the day she ever wanted to make that trip.

BOOM! BOOM! BOOM!

"Are you expecting anyone?" Bernard asked with a confused look on his face.

"No." Renee answers nervously.

BOOM! BOOM! BOOM!

"Do you want me to answer that for you?"

Looking over at her with a look of concern, because it was late and no one had called and stated they were on the way. And with his curiosity, he wanted to know if she had been seeing someone else besides him. For there could be a slight ounce of hope, that this baby wasn't his.

"Yeah, go ahead." Nudging him to get off the sofa. "So they can stop knocking like they the police or something." Rocking her newborn in her arms as she adjusted it for feeding.

Getting up from the sofa. Bernard looked out the window. But he couldn't see who it was because it was dark outside and Renee didn't have a porch light.

"Who is it?" He asked as he glared out the window at an unidentifiable shadow.

"Open this got damn door!" Shelly yelled. Using her foot to kick on the screen.

"Ahh shit, that's Shelly!" He whispered over at Renee antsy and anxious. In fear of what she might do to the both of them if she caught him there.

"Who!" Renee stated rhetorically. Shocked and nervous because she never expected Shelly to have been bold enough to pop up at her door step. She assumed Shelly was all talk and no action, but she was wrong. The day was neigh and she was standing fifteen feet away from where she sat. Ready to whop off in her ass.

"How she know where you live?" Questioning Renee angrily. Piercing her in the eyes with his imaginary evil eye ray beam.

"I don't fucking know!" Clutching the baby as if to use him as a shield. "I told you that bitch was crazy and you needed to leave her stupid ass alone!"

"How did she even know I was here?" Rushing to turn out the lights.

Renee said nothing as she sat on the sofa with a blank look on her face. No where to go. No where to run. Both him and Renee were trapped inside the house with only one exit and on the other side of that door stood a angry black woman. Renee didn't know much about Shelly, but she knew this wasn't going to end well. She had been provoking Shelly throughout her whole pregnancy and now that the baby was finally here. Shelly had no excuse on why she couldn't hit her. One thing that struck a sensitive nerve with Renee, was the fact that Shelly cleverly figured out her place of residency. And didn't have a clue on how she did it.

"She probably put a tracking device on your vehicle." Trying to place the blame on him. When she knew damn well it was her fault Shelly was at the door.

"Shut up!" He demanded. "She wouldn't do no shit like that. That's not even the type of woman she is. That's something you'd do."

"Open this got damn door!" She demanded with her left hand on her waist and her right pointing back and forth in the air as if she was waving a gun. "I know your ho ass in there bitch! And that bastard ass baby daddy of yours!" She shouted as the neighbors lights began to flick on one by one. "I saw you tried to turn out them lights! Like I wasn't going to notice! How stupid can you be?"

"What the hell!" He grumbled. "How she know about the baby ?" He blurts out belligerently. "How she knew you were pregnant? Hell… How she even know about you? Because I damn sure didn't tell her! And I don't leave my fucking phone laying around either!"

"I don't know!" Keeping a straight face as she lied. "She figured out where I stay! Ask her!"

"You been going threw my phone ain't you?" Making accusations now that the fire has gotten to hot for him. "Have you been calling her?"

"And if I did!" Now taking ownership of the part she played in this conspiracy. "You ain't going to do shit about it! So shut that shit up and handle that psycho at my door." Crossing her legs.

"What the fuck you been telling her?"

"I don't know why you ain't been told her about us. We a family! And she ain't got nothing to do with that!"

"FAMILY!" Looking at her as if she done lost her mind. "Bitch you ain't my family! You just some action and I got caught slipping!"

"You weren't saying that a few minutes ago. When you were begging me to put this pussy on your lip!"

"Fuck you bitch!"

"You did. See where that got you…"

Patients was not a quality Shelly was born with. Therefore, she grew tired of waiting on them to open up. She could hear them arguing back and forth with one another. Regarding, which of the two was the blame for her finding out about their fling. But, little did they both know. It didn't matter who did what. She was going to kick both their asses and she didn't have much time to let them decide. Because her fingers were going numb from the coldness of the night. This winter had been a cold bitch.

"Open this got damn door before I throw a brick threw this

motherfucking window!" Shelly could see a crowd beginning to form in the middle of the street. "Something coming through this mother fucker in 0.2 seconds! If you don't let me in this bitch!" More of the nosey neighbors have started coming out of their homes instead of continuing to peer out their windows.

"That's my wife out there!" Bernard argued. Frustrated with Renee's nonchalant behavior.

"YO WIFE!" Appalled. "Since when?" Wanting to lay the baby down. But she knew if she did that. She would be a breathing target. "And you wasn't screaming that shit when you was smelling and tasting this good shit nigga! Hell you talking bout!"

"See, all this shit you keep hollering about is pointless." Dismissing everything Renee was saying as if she never a word. "How long has she known?" Getting tired of her childish shenanigans.

"Ever since we left the Camions." With a devilish smirk on her face.

"What!" Realizing the light had shined on his infidelity months ago and his relationship with Shelly was completely over. "FUCK!" He yells as he punches the air as if there was a receiving opponent on the opposite side of his blow. "It's over now." He admits as he flopped down on the couch next to Renee. Placing his head in his hands as he tries to think of a way to get himself clear of this situation. It was one thing for his career to be flushed down the drain. But, it felt even worse to be loosing the woman you loved and stuck with a baby mama. Busted and disgusted he thought. The story of his life. From fame to shame.

BOOM! BOOM! BOOM!

"Open up bitch!" Shelly continued to bully. "You just texted me and now you want to act all scared cause you didn't think I would pull up on yo block and come unglued on that ass!" Beating on the door. "Well bitch! I warned you. I don't play childish games! You hear! I'd knock yo block off bitch, open up!" Getting antsy Shelly started realizing, they weren't going to open the door. "You know what, fuck both y'all ducks!" Turning to walk down the stairs and get back in her car. She had to find a way to relieve herself of some of this rage she felt somehow. "My blood pressure ain't go up for nothing." She said. Making her way to her vehicle. Shelly took a good look around the front yard. Trying to see if she could find just one good sized rock to launch threw the living room. But she had no luck. "They lucked up this time, but I got something for that ass!" Grinning at the cleaver scheme she thought up in her mind.

Going to the rear of her truck. Shelly reached into her back pocket in search of her keys. Once the trunk was popped, she grabbed her crow bar. Slamming the trunk back shut. She kindly made her way to the middle of both vehicles in the driveway. And made sure both their tires were flattened before she left.

"That'll show em." Feeling a little satisfaction after leaving her signature mark of evidence that she'd been there.

She started up the car and royally rolled over the mailbox while making her exit.

"Bitches!" She yelled loud enough for them to hear her echo.

Once Shelly got back to Bernard's house. She started packing her things. In the mist of packing, she received continuous phone calls from him. But she never answered or read any of the messages he sent as well. The only thing she knew was her relationship with Bernard Curry had been a lie from day one, and her life would fall into bigger pieces if she stayed. Stuffing her things in the truck. Shelly realized she'd never told anyone the plans she'd made in regard to leaving Bernard. Not even her own sister knew what was going on between the two. With all the money she stashed away in one of

Jasmines suitcases, she'd kept to remember her by. Shelly knew that she and her unborn child would be taken good care of. Defiantly, with Michael being the father.

*

*

QUESTIONS

1. What did you expect from the book when you first read the title?
2. Was Shelly's story shocking, or could you anticipate what the outcome would be?
3. Do you consider Jasmine to have been a 'true' friend to Shelly?
4. How did you feel when Jasmine confessed to Shelly about what happened between her and Bernard?
5. Who was your favorite character? Why?
6. Have you ever been betrayed? If so, did you forgive them or could you ever forgive them?
7. What did you make of Renee?
8. Did the ending catch you by surprise?
9. Which character best duplicate your personality? Is that a good thing?
10. Would you read this again?

ABOUT THE AUTHOR

Born and raised in Atlanta, Georgia. Danielle Walker has always strived to become an entrepreneur since the early age of eight. It started with odd jobs around the house, which soon led to braiding hair for extra cash. Becoming a Corporate Lawyer has always been a dream of hers, but it soon changed in her early semesters of college. Where she had the opportunity to intern for one of Atlanta's most prestigious law firms 'The Mosby Law Group'.

Seeing and experiencing first hand the hectic-ness of running a law firm. Danielle decided that particular career field wasn't for her. Continuing to work two jobs and maintain being a full-time student. Danielle eventually realized working extremely hard wasn't something she wanted to do either. Later she found herself at a crossroad because she didn't have a plan B.

With life experiences having their way with her and her motivation to make something of herself at it's peek. Danielle picked up her pen and did what she felt came natural to her. Today Ms. Walker is the owner of 'YJLM Publishing House' and is the author of one of the best selling books of 2014. Optimistic for the future, you can guarantee she is ready to take on her next challenge in life. One day at a time.